MW01034178

GHOST DETECTIVE

Zachary Muswagon

ESCHIA
BOOKS

© 2012 by Eschia Books Inc.
First printed in 2012 10 9 8 7 6 5 4 3 2 1
Printed in Canada

All rights reserved. No part of this work covered by the copyrights
hereon may be reproduced or used in any form or by any means—
graphic, electronic or mechanical—without the prior written permission
of the publisher, except for reviewers, who may quote brief passages.
Any request for photocopying, recording, taping or storage on
information retrieval systems of any part of this work shall be
directed in writing to the publisher.

The Publisher: Eschia Books Inc.

Library and Archives Canada Cataloguing in Publication

Muswagon, Zachary
Ghost detective / Zachary Muswagon.

ISBN 978-1-926696-20-1

I. Title.

PS8626.U85G56 2012   C813'.6   C2012-904237-4

Project Director: Kathy van Denderen
Cover Image: woods background: © andreiuc88 / shutterstock
crow: © LHF Graphics / shutterstock

Produced with the assistance of the Government of Alberta, **Government**
Alberta Multimedia Development Fund   **of Alberta** ■

We acknowledge the support of the Canada Council for the Arts,
which last year invested $154 million to bring the arts to Canadians
throughout the country.

 Canada Council   Conseil des Arts
for the Arts   du Canada

PC: 1

Dedication

To the memory of Darren Zenko

Prologue

Bear looked at Crow perched on the tree branch above him. He waved a meaty paw in the bird's direction.

"You owe me, buddy," Bear said. His voice was a low, deep growl, like the sound of a broken-down Harley-Davidson.

Crow laughed, a sound like Woody Woodpecker's older and meaner brother. "I owe you nothing! I won that hand fair and square."

"If *fair* means dealing from the bottom of the deck, then I guess you did. But in most circles it doesn't. So you owe me."

The bird hopped down to a lower branch, close enough so he could see the bear better but far enough away from those giant paws. Crow wasn't taking any chances. Bears looked slow and dumpy—this one liked to lumber around more than your average bear—but bears could catch you unawares, exploding in a rage of fur, claws and teeth, faster than lightning.

You had to be careful around bears, even the ones who seemed friendly.

"I don't know why you're making a big deal out of this," Crow said, flapping his wings. "You weren't even playing the hand. You went into the woods to do whatever it is that bears do in the woods. It wasn't even your money that was lost. It was Coyote's."

Bear sat down, crushing a bush beneath his giant furry butt.

"Yeah, Coyote," Bear said quietly. "He was pretty angry that he lost. I heard he went out afterward and razed a couple of chicken coops." Bear extended a single sharp claw, half the size of the bird's entire body, and started to pick his teeth. "Didn't even eat the chickens, just snapped their necks and left their tiny, broken little bodies strewn all over the yard. Feathers and blood everywhere; not a pretty sight. Not a pretty sight."

Bear picked a piece of meat out of his teeth, looked at the morsel for a second and then popped it back into his mouth. "It would be a shame if Coyote found out that your dealing wasn't as honest as he thought it was. He'd probably be even angrier than when he had killed all those poor chickens."

Crow puffed up his feathers. "Y-y-y, you wouldn't d-d-dare," the bird sputtered. "You wouldn't dare tell him. We're supposed to be friends."

Bear erupted from his sitting position, claws flaying, teeth gnashing. He tore branches from the tree. A raging roar burst from his throat.

Even though he was far enough from the bear to be safe, the bird's natural instinct kicked in, triggering a hurried flight reaction. By the time Crow came to his senses, he found himself at the top of the tree, his tiny heart pounding so hard his chest feathers were bouncing.

He looked down at Bear, who was still raging, his front claws ripping the tree's bark in foot-long chunks and his back paws flinging massive mounds of dirt behind him. "You told the boy I had the Chinook!" Bear roared. "You told the boy I stole the Chinook, you lousy bird, and because of that, I have to sleep through the entire winter, cold and dark in my den."

Crow remembered a time long ago, when Bear had stolen the Chinook, the warm wind that brings the spring. Crow knew Bear had stolen spring because they had been in on it together. It was the biggest heist in the history of the world. That's why Crow went along with the plan. Sure, he would have stayed warm and dry all year long, never having to scrounge in the thick snow for cold berries, frozen mice or dead plants. But it was the audacity of the whole heist that had attracted him—the thrill of the steal.

But Bear kept the Chinook to himself, hiding it in a buffalo-skin bag at the back of his den. He didn't want to share the warmth of the Chinook, not with anyone, not even with his friend who helped steal it. That's how much Bear hated the cold.

So Crow told the boy, who along with Coyote and Prairie Chicken had stolen the Chinook back. And because of that, spring would always come, but since then Bear had to sleep in his den all winter.

Crow knew Bear hated to hibernate because he hated to be out of the loop for such a long time. Bear hated not knowing what was going on. Crow also found it funny that Bear still held a grudge, even though the event with the Chinook happened so long ago.

The bird waited at the top of the tree until Bear wore himself out and fell back down on his ass. Bear's head slumped forward onto his chest, and he was breathing heavily.

Crow slowly drifted down to a lower branch of the tree. He knew Bear was tired, so he didn't need to worry about an attack.

"I can't believe you're still angry about that," Crow said, tilting his head to the side. "It's your own damn fault, and you know it."

Bear sighed and nodded. "Yeah, I know, I know. I'm sorry. Just forget about it."

"So you're not going to tell Coyote about the cards?" Crow asked.

"No, I'm not going to tell him. He's a jerk and deserves it if somebody like you cheats him," Bear said. "I was just so desperate because of the family thing involved in this."

"You mean the incident with your grandson?"

Bear nodded, tears starting to stream from his eyes.

Now this is something different, Crow thought. He had never seen Bear cry, and they had known each other for a long time.

"This is important to you," Crow said.

Bear nodded, but it was such a slow and deep nod that it seemed the entire earth moved with his head. "It's one of the most important things facing my people since, well... since the Europeans came."

"That *is* important," said Crow. The bird began to think about all the ways and reasons to say no to Bear's request, but he just couldn't think of anything. No reason was enough to say no.

"Okay," Crow said. "I'll do it."

Bear looked up, a mix of surprise and gratitude lighting up his face. "You mean it? You'll really do it?"

The bird nodded. "Why not?" And to show how serious he was, he flew over to Bear and settled on his shoulder, within easy reach of those sharps claws and teeth. "Tell me about the boy."

Bear smiled as bears do, with his eyes, not his mouth. He pushed up from the sitting position onto his four paws. And with Crow still on his shoulder, Bear walked toward the other world. "His name is Billy," he started.

PART I

One

Billy Ghostkeeper woke to the sound of a screeching crow. The sound grated on his ears, scraping on his eardrums and then digging deeper into his brain. The pain it created was intense, like someone had drilled a hole into his forehead, right through to the back.

Billy hadn't felt such pain in his head since the last time he had gotten drunk. *Dammit*, he thought to himself as the pain kept slicing into him. *Thirteen years sober ruined in one lousy night.*

He tried to recall what had happened the night before that led to his fall off the wagon, but he couldn't remember. That wasn't too surprising; he was prone to blackouts when he used to drink, but this time was different. Usually he had something to go on, snippets of conversation, visual images of the places he'd been or the people who had been there, the smell and taste of beer, smokes and vomit.

But he had nothing, absolutely nothing, no memory of anything from the last twenty-four hours. It was like he had a giant hole in his head, and the only thing his mind could pick up on was the squawking of that damn crow.

He reached down to pull the covers over his head to try to drown out the sound of the bird but realized he didn't have a blanket. *Probably fell on the floor.*

He reached out for his quilt, the handmade one from his aunt, but instead of feeling the air above the floor, he came upon something soft and a bit wet. It felt like warm Jell-O, but gritty, as if it had grains of sand dispersed through it.

He figured the goo was probably the remnants of the contents of his stomach following his night of debauchery. Disgusted, he flicked the stuff away and placed his hands over his ears. If he could stop the sound of that damn bird, then maybe the pain would fade and he could get some sleep before he had to go back to his life and apologize for his drunken carousing to anyone who needed to be apologized to.

In the old days when he drank, that list could be long.

But no matter how hard he pressed his hands against his ears, or even if he stuck a finger into each of them, the crow's screams only got louder. It became so intense that Billy finally had to sit up.

"Will you shut up!" he shouted at the bird. His voice felt distant, as if it wasn't even there. And the physical act of sitting up and shouting drained Billy of all his energy. His vision blurred, his head swam and an immense fatigue flowed into his body, reaching deep inside, through the muscles right into the marrow of his bones.

He fell back to a prone position but realized that the crow had stopped screeching. At least something was going his way today.

"Think again, buddy," a voice said, as if reading Billy's mind. It was a high-pitched, gravely voice. Billy recalled a comedian, small and annoying, who had imitated a bird's voice in some cartoon, but he couldn't think of his name.

He opened his eyes to see who or what had made that sound. Big mistake! The light was intense. To call it a blinding glare was the understatement of the century. It burned into his retinas, flared up his optic nerves like a fuse raging up a line of gunpowder and set his visual cortex on fire. The pain radiated through the rest of his brain, pushing out through that hole in his head he had felt earlier.

Somehow, though, and he didn't know how, he could see something. It bounced in front of the light, a tiny shadow, shaped like a bird, sitting on a branch above Billy. Was it a crow? It seemed to look at him quizzically. And then it flew away.

"Great," Billy said to himself, "I didn't even make it home." But again, that had happened to him before when he used to drink. It was one of the reasons he stopped drinking. One of the many.

He shut his eyes against the glare and roughly rubbed them. His body was telling him to sleep so he decided not to fight it. And with that crow now gone, he could.

He rolled over onto his side, throwing his right arm out like he always did since he was a kid. His arm hit something soft, and the instant it did, Billy knew exactly what it was. Ending up in bed with a stranger was another symptom of his drinking. But something was wrong with the body next to him. It was cold. And not cold like there aren't any covers around, but cold like death.

Billy yanked his hand away in horror. And even though he was exhausted, he pushed himself to a sitting position again. He opened his eyes to the same intense light and stared at the body next to him.

What he saw knocked him onto his back again; his brain wasn't able to make any sense of the scene before him. His neurons were firing, but they couldn't make a connection between what was supposed to be and what he had just seen. So his brain shut down.

But before Billy fell back into oblivion, he heard the crow screeching again.

Two

Billy dreamed of a sweat. And not just any sweat. It was the first sweat his Mosum had invited him to participate in. Not only was he allowed to be part of the sweat, but Billy also helped to make the lodge.

One morning, Mosum took him into the garage. It was typically full of the bric-a-brac found in garages, the junk of life that people collect, jammed into boxes or shoved into dark corners and unused rooms, to be forgotten.

A small Japanese-made pickup with its wheels exposed was sitting up on blocks. More junk was piled up in the box of the truck, various bits of old carpet, tarps and blankets.

Billy, who was about thirteen at the time, followed Mosum through the junk in the garage, heading toward the back. Mosum was a bear of a man, over six-and-a-half-feet tall, at least two-hundred-and-fifty pounds or more, and his lumbering movements knocked over a bunch of the stuff as he plowed a path through the junk. But he didn't care; he just kept on going.

"Bears are the top predator wherever they live," Mosum growled when Billy tried to pick up the fallen bits and put them back in their proper places. "They don't worry about what they knock over when they walk. So leave those things alone."

So Billy stepped over the items Mosum knocked over and continued to walk to the door that led to the backyard. Along one garage wall was a large metal tub, about eight-feet long, filled with water. Soaking in the water were several birch saplings, each one about six-feet long. Mosum reached into the tub and pulled out two of the saplings. He laid the two branches on the cement floor with the top points, small branches reaching out like baby fingers, facing toward each other; the thicker ends, where they had been cut, facing out.

"This is what I want you to do," Mosum said, pulling the smaller ends together so that they overlapped by about a foot and a half. "Pretty easy and won't take you long."

Mosum stepped on the two saplings to hold them together on the ground and looked around. His eyes found what he was searching for, and he jerked his chin up and pursed his lips at the messy workbench behind them. Billy turned and saw all sorts tools and materials. "Hand me that roll of twine and those scissors," Mosum said. So Billy did.

Mosum unrolled a long section of twine, cut it with the scissors—dropping the tool on the ground with a small clang—and then bent down and lashed the two saplings together to make one pole about twelve-feet long. He shook the pole to test the strength of his knots, and though the saplings bowed and bounced, they held together.

Mosum dropped the pole on the cement floor, and with pursed lips he pointed at the other saplings in the tub of water and handed Billy the roll of twine.

"Lash the rest of these saplings together, but watch the water 'cause it's cold, and make sure you tie them together strong, but with some give, like that one I just did. Try to keep them the same length, or at least close to the same length. At this time of year, they're pretty brittle after you cut them down 'cause of the cold. They've been soaking for a couple of days to make them more flexible. But take it easy—one or two of them might still be brittle. We can afford to break one, but if two or three break, we've got a problem. Sounds easy, right?"

Billy nodded, looking into the tub and seeing about ten or so saplings left, enough to make five or six long poles.

"It's not rocket science, but this is only one part of what I need you to do today." He waved a hand at Billy to step back. He picked up the pole he had made and headed out the door.

"When you're done with all of them, bring them outside, along with the twine and the scissors, and we'll work on the rest of today's job."

When his Mosum left, Billy reached into the water and grabbed the first sapling. The water was so cold that it felt like his skin was burning. But the cold wasn't that bad because his hands weren't in the water long and the garage was slightly heated. It wasn't a difficult job, just a bit awkward with the long saplings.

Billy took his time, working deliberately and thoroughly so he wouldn't break any of the saplings. He tied the rest of the poles together progressively faster, getting a sense of the flexibility of the wood and being satisfied with their lengths.

Every so often, a blast of noise came from the backyard. It sounded like a gas lawn mower starting up, and then it whined like a drill bit cutting into a thick piece of wood and then it stopped. The noise repeated about ten times.

Billy constructed five poles, leaving a lone sapling in the tub. They were light, and he tried to pick them up from the ground, but they were too unwieldy to carry all at once. He made two trips to the backyard. It was there he discovered what was making the noise.

Mosum had a portable gas auger, one normally used to make holes for ice fishing, but the bit on this auger was small, only a couple of inches in diameter. Mosum was using the auger to drill a series of holes into the ground forming a large circle around another roughly dug hole. Mosum was using the sapling pole he had lashed together as a measuring stick for the diameter of the circle. He had also stacked a pile of stones, each about the size of a head of lettuce, off to one side.

By the time Billy had placed all the saplings in a pile near the circle, Mosum had finished drilling. He set the auger down and came over to inspect Billy's work. He checked the strength of the knots and the flexibility of the poles the same way he had checked his own, by lifting it up in the middle and shaking the pole to ensure it would bounce.

"Good job," he said, nodding in satisfaction. "Now, did you see that old pickup in the garage?"

Billy nodded.

"In the box there's a bunch of junk, mostly pieces of carpet, tarps and blankets. We're going to need them at some point, but right now I need some carpet laid down in this circle. Don't cover the big hole, but you can overlap the circle if you have to, okay?"

Billy nodded, and he did as he was told. The carpet scraps were dusty, and he had coughing fits while arranging the carpet, but in no time, he made a nice circular layer of carpet on the ground.

"Right," Mosum said, grabbing one of the saplings and slowly turning and pointing one of the ends toward Billy. "Take this end and stick it in one of the holes."

Billy did as he was told, and the pole snapped upward as Mosum let go of his end.

Mosum walked to the pile of stones and picked up two. He dropped one stone near Billy and set the other one on the opposite end of the circle. Mosum stepped into the circle and reached up to grab the sapling. "You got that in the hole pretty good?" he asked.

Billy looked down to make sure his end was secure and then nodded. "Yep, it's okay."

"Right." Slowly, but with assurance, Mosum bent the sapling, taking his end and sticking it into the opposite hole so that the pole arched over the ring of carpet. He slid his rock over and set it on the outer part of the post to keep it in place. He didn't need to tell Billy that he had to do the same.

"Everything secure?" he asked. Billy nodded. "Okay, slowly lift your hand from your end."

Billy slowly let go, and while the pole stretched outward, his end stayed in the hole, braced by the rock.

Mosum nodded and pointed at the pile of sapling poles. "Grab another one and hand me the other end." They repeated the process, but positioned this pole at a ninety-degree angle from the other pole so that two arches intersected in an "X."

Again, they braced the pole with rocks. Mosum held the two poles together where they intersected. "Hold this," he said, and Billy stepped up, grabbing the two poles. Mosum picked up the roll of twine and the scissors. With deft quickness, he lashed the two arches together at the "X."

"Figure out what we're making?" Mosum asked as he tied a series of complicated knots.

"We're making a sweat lodge."

Mosum smiled but said nothing. A smile from his Mosum was all Billy needed to feel good.

"Is the sweat lodge just for you, or can I use it?" Billy asked tentatively.

"Well, that's the whole point of this exercise, isn't it? I didn't bring you out here just to be cheap labor and then send you home. Anybody can participate in a sweat—I mean, there are plenty of guys around that have some nice lodges that I could have taken you to, but it's much better to do a sweat in a lodge that you've built yourself. Can't explain it. It's something you have to experience for yourself to get what

I'm talking about. And you're old enough now. No point in me talking about you getting in touch with your culture if I don't show you, am I right?"

Mosum tied a final knot and snipped the twine from the roll. "Okay, let those puppies go, but do it slowly."

The arches stretched upward, and the poles didn't break. They all held together. Billy felt satisfaction at seeing all the pieces turn into a structure. It didn't look like much now, just two arches over a circle, but it was the beginning of the sweat lodge, a place that could not only protect them from the cold and wind, but it was also a spiritual place. And Billy felt good about it.

But then Billy realized that Mosum was no longer beside him. Somehow he had left without Billy seeing or hearing him. He looked about, wondering if his Mosum had gone into the garage, but when he turned around, the house and garage were gone.

"Mosum!" he called out. He called out again and again, every time a little louder until he was shouting.

"MOSUM!"

There was no response, save for the sound of the wind through the branches. Billy was all alone in the middle of the circle, wondering what he should do next.

And then a crow landed on the top of the arch. The bird ruffled its feathers, and after a moment, began squawking at him.

Three

When Billy woke again, the crow was perched on his chest. It wasn't doing anything threatening. The bird just stood there, head cocked to the side, giving Billy a quizzical look. Even so, the closeness of the bird surprised Billy, and he immediately thought the animal was going to peck out his eyes.

So he jumped up, screaming, "Get away from me! Get away from me!" his arms flaying in the air.

The bird fluttered away, settling above Billy on the branch of a nearby tree. After a pause, the crow squawked at him. The sound pierced through Billy's skull, knocking him back, making him stagger and drop onto one knee. Even in his haze of pain, Billy thought, this is not a normal hangover.

The bird squawked again so Billy reached down, scooped up a clump of dirt and flung it at the bird. His headache was so intense that he didn't see where the dirt landed, but since the bird screamed again, he figured he must have missed his target.

Billy grabbed another clump of dirt and threw it at the bird.

This time, he heard a small fleshy bump and an exhalation of air, as if he hit something. Or somebody.

"Hey, what's the big idea?" a voice grunted. "I was only trying to help."

Billy looked around quickly, his body spinning to the left and right, searching for the source of the voice. "Who's there?" he stammered. "Who is it?"

"Stop being an idiot. Nobody's here," the voice said. "It's just me."

Billy slowly turned to the sound of the voice. He didn't see anyone, just the crow sitting on a branch, shaking some dirt from his feathers. Billy shook his head.

"Great, Billy. See what happens when you fall off the wagon?" Billy said to himself. "You start to go crazy and hear crows talk."

The bird screeched again, but this time the noise didn't increase the pain in Billy's head. The crow flew off the branch and landed on the ground about ten feet in front of Billy. The bird hopped once toward him.

"You're not going crazy," the bird said. "You're just an idiot."

"Holy shit!" Billy screamed, backpedaling away and holding up his hands in front of his face. He tripped on something and tumbled backward, slipping down a slight rise and landing in a creek that cut through a patch of trees. The shock of the freezing water stunned him for a moment. The back of his head hit some stones at the bottom of the creek, and he saw a flash of light and felt pain. Billy blacked out just for a second, but when water ran into his nose and mouth, and then into his lungs, his survival instinct kicked in. He started thrashing against the water, trying to pull himself up out of the creek to stop from drowning. But he couldn't escape. The stones in the creek were too slippery, and the water ran too fast. The water was going to overwhelm him. He didn't think he would make it.

"Stand up!" the crow shouted. "It's not deep."

Billy thrashed for a while longer before the voice registered in his brain. He wasn't trapped in a deep, raging river after all, just a slow-moving creek. As soon as he stopped struggling and stood up, he saw the water was barely up to his knees.

Sheepishly, he walked out of the creek. Oddly enough, he didn't seem to be that wet, and the water was no longer cold. What was even odder was that he had taken the advice of a crow.

Billy looked about and spotted the bird sitting on a branch jutting out over the creek. It hopped along the branch until it was within a few feet of Billy.

"You know, your grandfather said you were a good kid," the bird said. "But sometimes you aren't that bright. I can see that your Mosum was pretty accurate in his description of you."

"Mosum?" Billy said to himself, remembering the old man who had taught him many things. In his head he heard Mosum's growling voice. "There are many strange and wonderful beings in the world. And sometimes they will talk to you. And even if you think it's the craziest idea in the world, it's best that you talk to them. You might learn something important."

"What the heck is going on?" Billy asked the crow. "And where the hell am I?"

The crow nodded. "Ahh, excellent. Two very good questions. Questions that can be taken in many ways. They can be specific questions, in which the query is about the specific nature of the situation, and specific answers about the localized situation are needed. But at the same time," said the bird as he pointed one wing in the air, "these questions also have an existential nature seeking to determine the meaning of life, the universe and everything."

The bird dropped his wing and turned to Billy. "However, based on my brief experience with you, I think it's safe to assume that you're not the kind of guy who really cares about the existential nature of himself, and you're more keen to know what the heck is going on, right here, right now. Am I right?"

Billy's head still hurt a bit, but it had nothing to do with a hangover. "Who *are* you?" he asked the bird, ignoring the question.

"Another excellent question. To be honest, I don't have time to give you the full answer," the bird said in a tone that sounded almost insulting. "And I don't think you'd really get even one percent of what I'd be describing anyway. So I'm going to keep it really simple. I am your spirit guide," the crow said, puffing out his chest and feathers with pride.

"Huh?" Billy looked at the bird, dazed. And then he said, "I thought my spirit guide was a bear?"

The crow thumped one wing against the branch. It seemed like the act of petulant child, but it was hard to tell. "No, no. Your spirit guide is a bird—a crow to be exact. Not a bear."

"But Mosum told me my spirit guide was a bear. It doesn't make any sense."

The crow sighed in exasperation. "Well, if it was a bear, then you'd be talking to a bear. Or at least trying to because bears aren't that bright. But at the moment, you're talking to a crow, which should tell you what animal your spirit guide is."

"But how can that be? Ghostkeepers are bears. We've always been bears."

"Only some of you are bears. Every family has many sides, and parts of your family are crows. Another part porcupines, but if you ask me, you really shouldn't hang around those types. They're too low to the ground."

"But why are you here now? All my life I've been waiting for a spirit guide to help me. I've been asking, even praying, for one to appear all my life. Mosum said they were out there, just waiting for us to call upon them."

The crow squawked, and Billy thought it sounded like laughter. "We may be 'out there,' boy, but we're not at your beck and call. We animals have busy lives, surviving and all, looking out for predators, so we can't always come when you call," the bird said. "And besides, I've been there for you many times, calling to you and trying to show you the way, but you never noticed me. You were too preoccupied with the trappings of the real world to pay me any attention. Of course, you being a crow, that's kind of a given. We like shiny things."

Billy realized he did like shiny new objects: his truck always had to be clean, and he had to have the biggest flatscreen TV on the Rez with the most powerful subwoofers and surround-sound speakers. Even as a kid, he had to have the newest toys he saw on TV commercials. It drove his parents crazy.

"Yeah, but why now?" Billy asked. "Why can I see you now and not before?"

"Well, a person usually has to experience some major trauma in life before they're open to their spirit guide. Or some life-changing event. And in your case," the bird said, pointing a wing at the ground to Billy's right, "nothing's more life-changing than death."

Billy turned and looked in the direction the bird pointed. He gasped, bringing his hand to his mouth when he saw the body. His stomach lurched, and the piercing pain in his head returned. He remembered a recent image, the sight that had brought about his blackout and the dream of his grandfather. This time, though, Billy didn't pass out; he just looked at the body in stunned silence.

It was a male, early thirties, wearing a pair of jeans that had once been pressed but now were wrinkled and covered in dirt. The shirt was black with embroidered Western designs above each pocket. The man's mouth was open and so were his eyes, empty like an overcast night sky but with a hint of surprise. A trail of dried blood came from the small hole in the center of his forehead. A couple of ants darted around the hole.

Billy knew instantly what had caused the hole— a bullet. He also knew the hole at the back of the man's head would be much larger and messier.

"He's dead," Billy said. "Somebody killed him."

The crow flew off the branch and landed on Billy's shoulder. Billy barely felt the bird's presence and didn't bat him away.

"Wrong pronouns," the bird said quietly.

It took a second before Billy realized what the bird was talking about.

Four

Kena Ghostkeeper was sitting in her living room and watching TV. She loved TV; it was one of the white man's greatest inventions. Of course, she heard from many of the younger, more militant generation that the white man used TV as a means to control the people they wanted to control, like the blacks or the Indians or poor white folks.

Kena wasn't an idiot; she understood that line of thinking, but rich white folks watched a lot of TV too because so many TV shows were about them. You'd figure, she thought, that if TV was designed to control folks like her, or blacks or white trailer trash, you'd see more of them on TV. But mostly the shows were about rich white folks, which she didn't mind.

And she knew that TV kept a lot of people, including herself, from going outside, especially kids. But with her legs hurting all the time with the diabetes, it was tough for her to even walk to the bathroom sometimes. Soon she'd have to get one of those walkers like she saw the old white folks on TV using.

But the main reason Kena Ghostkeeper liked to watch TV was that it kept the spirits and their annoying voices at bay.

Kena was rare among her people. She had the "Eyes of Fire," the ability to see and talk to all the spirits of the lands—the animals, the plants, the dead and not so dead. She could see signs that pointed the way to the future or what could be the future. She could see inside a person, see their colors and their lights and discover why they were sick or feeling out of sorts. She could see the invisible "travois" that every one of her people carried and see whether the load they carried held them back or moved them forward. She could go on vision quests that took her much deeper and farther than anyone else she knew, even reaching into the world where the Creator and the old ones lived. She was a shaman, a spiritual guide, a healer, an elder of great power, respected by her people.

And her abilities annoyed the living shit out of her.

Kena remembered the day long ago when she discovered she had the Eyes of Fire. She had been a typical little girl, running around and playing games with her friends. But one of the priests at school had noticed that several of her playmates were imaginary. Of course, it was normal for most kids to have imaginary friends. But after awhile, those friends go away as kids get older.

That was not the case with Kena. By the time she was in grade five, she still talked to her imaginary friends, who, to her, weren't really imaginary when compared to the "real" friends she hung out with in school. Her imaginary friends were just different.

But then the priest noticed Kena talking to herself, and one day he called her into his office. He invited her to sit down, a rare thing, and he pulled his chair close to her, as if she was offering confession. He asked her if she was praying when she was talking to herself. When she said no, that she was talking to her friends, the priest frowned.

"These friends of yours do not exist," he said to Kena. "They are not real." When he said the word *friends*, his voice had a strange tone, like he was saying one of those words Kena had heard the older kids say. Bad words that started with the letters "F" or "S."

She told the priest that of course they were real. They were her friends, different from the others but still real.

The priest's face turned bright red. His voice was tight as he explained again that her friends were *not* real. Good people did not talk to imaginary friends or hear voices telling them what to do.

"What about Jesus?" she asked him innocently. "You've said he was the best person who ever lived. And he heard and talked to the voice of God and the Holy Spirit. And so did Mary and Joseph. They talked to angels. Moses too. God was a burning bush to him. Maybe it's like that for me?"

Kena wasn't expecting the priest to hit her. But he did. He struck her across the face, knocking her off the chair. And then he picked her up off the floor, shouting. "You are nothing like Jesus! You are a savage beast, and the spirits you claim to talk to are the voices of the devil!" And then he hit her again.

Kena didn't remember what happened to her after that. She woke up later in her bed, her face stinging with pain. But what hurt worse was the shame, the shame of being called a savage, the shame of hearing the voices of the devil who said they were her friends. The voices never told her to do anything wrong or to hurt anybody so she had thought they were her friends. But since the priest had told her she was wrong in speaking to them, she must have been wrong. They had taken her from her home and family to go to this special school, so the priest must be right.

It was only when she went home for the summer that she found out the truth. It wasn't entirely unusual for someone to return home from the special school quiet and sad. But Kena was sadder than most.

Finally, her grandmother noticed. "Kena, my little dear," her Kokum said in Cree. "You seem so sad these days. What's wrong?"

Kena knew she shouldn't listen to people talking Cree; that's what they told her in school. But Kokum couldn't speak English. The school also taught Kena to respect her elders, especially the priests and the nuns, so Kena was a bit confused. In the end, she decided to talk to her Kokum. She tried to explain in English but finally had to speak Cree. Kena found it difficult to remember the language, but she finally got the words out and told her story.

Kena was expecting her Kokum to get angry like the priest had been, but instead the old lady smiled. She hugged Kena. "You are special," her grandmother said. And then she took Kena to her parents. When they heard the news, they were also happy and hugged Kena.

Kena's parents took her to an old auntie that Kena had never met before. This woman was supposed to have been her Kokum's great aunt, so Kena knew the woman was probably the oldest person in the world.

"Leave her with me," the auntie said to Kena's parents and her Kokum when they told her the story.

The auntie asked Kena a bunch of questions about her friends and the voices she heard. She asked Kena if she saw light coming from some people, and Kena said yes. The old woman poked and prodded Kena in various ways, like the school's doctor did, but unlike the doctor, the auntie was gentle and loving. And then the auntie looked deeply into Kena's eyes for a long time. It was like Kena was looking into a long hole, but one that was filled with light and color and joy.

Finally the old auntie gave a grunt and a nod. And she called in Kena's parents and Kokum.

"She has the Eyes of Fire," the auntie said.

Kena's parents and Kokum exploded with happiness, squeezing the young girl in the strongest hugs they had ever given. Kena had never felt happier in her life.

In the joy of the moment, Kena looked up and saw the auntie smiling at her. The aunt's eyes sparkled with delight but had a tinge of sadness as well. "It is a great gift," she told Kena in a voice that no one else could hear but her. "But you must never tell the white man about it. And you must realize that while you will be able to help your people, the gift can be annoying. Sometimes you will never be left alone, even when you are by yourself."

The old auntie's statement echoed in Kena's head as she settled in to watch another TV episode of rich white girls living in New York City. The voices and spirits were becoming insistent these days with many more children's voices than usual. She had no idea how to respond to their persistent requests for help.

Before, she had healed them and sent them on their way—just like she would do to her neighbors, the live people who came to her with a variety of ailments. That's why she had the Eyes of Fire, to be a healer. But when she was diagnosed with diabetes, she realized that everything she had told her neighbors about living right and finding balance in the world had meant nothing. Getting diabetes meant she had failed the most important person a healer could fail: herself. And if she couldn't take care and heal herself, how could she claim to heal others? So Kena just turned up the volume of the TV to drown out the voices of the dead and the feelings of guilt in her head.

Five

Billy Ghostkeeper stumbled along a dusty gravel road. His mind was a mix of confused thoughts and emotions; he frantically waved his arms in the air as he walked.

"Dead!? How can I be dead?" he shouted to the sky. "I'm too young to die. I haven't even hit forty yet. I'm supposed to live another fifty years, and by then they'll have longevity treatments that'll keep me alive for another three hundred years. It's not fair. It's just not fair!"

Billy stopped walking and began to stomp around in a circle like a petulant child. He screamed and raged, bent down to the ground and scooped up two handfuls of gravel and flung it up into the air. The gravel rained down on him, some of the tiny rocks striking him in the face and the dust slipping into his mouth down into his lungs and choking him.

He collapsed into a hack attack, his hands grabbing at his throat in pain, the coughing and retching jerking his body back and forth. After he calmed down, he paused, looked around him and then laughed manically.

"Ha! I knew I wasn't dead," he said, sitting down in the middle of the road. "If I was dead, then I shouldn't have felt the rocks and the dust in my lungs. I *must* be alive."

The crow suddenly appeared and fluttered down and landed in front of Billy. "Face it, kid. You're dead. No ifs, ands or buts about it," the bird said, sadly shaking his head.

"No. I disagree." Billy raised his index finger in the air. "*If* I was dead, I shouldn't have been able to pick up that gravel and throw it. *And…*" he raised a second finger, "the rocks and the dust shouldn't have made me cough." He held up three fingers in the air. "*But* it did. So therefore I am not dead."

The crow looked at him and raised a wing into the air. "So how do you explain the body in the ravine, the one that looks like you? And how do you explain *me*? How do you explain a talking crow?"

"Easy. I'm either dreaming or hallucinating."

"Pretty vivid dream, if ask me."

"I've had them before," Billy said. "When I was a kid. I would dream of flying, hovering above the trees like a bird."

"Any birds talk to you in those dreams?"

"No," Billy said quietly.

"How about dead bodies that look like you? Any of that?"

Billy looked up at the sky. After a pause, he said, "No. No dead bodies."

"So none of this stuff has ever happened to you before?"

"I'm not dead!" Billy snatched up some gravel and threw it at the bird. The crow easily dodged the rocks by flying away. "I can't be dead! I'm too young to die!"

The bird fluttered down and landed on the same spot in the road in front of Billy. "This is typical, Billy. Everyone who dies goes through this. Denial is a classic step in the stages of death. It's actually stage three."

"Seriously? You're going to feed me that crap about stages of death? I mean...you're talking to an expert about stages and steps, you know. I had to go through twelve of them to get sober."

"That's good," the bird said, hopping back and forth as if pacing. "Then you'll be able to get through this stage much faster. You're already at the denial stage, and soon you'll be at the acceptance stage."

"And what happens at the acceptance stage?" Billy asked sarcastically. "I see a long tunnel with a light at the end and go into it?"

The bird squawked a couple of times, like he was laughing. "Ha. That's funny, Billy. A long tunnel with a light. Everybody knows that's just a hallucination brought on by your brain being starved by oxygen."

"Aha," Billy said raising a finger in the air. "Then how do we know my brain isn't being starved of oxygen right now and causing this whole hallucination? Maybe that explains all of this."

The bird stopped hopping and looked at Billy. It seemed to Billy that the crow was almost smiling.

"Excellent, that shows that you're getting really close to acceptance, that you're willing to accept that you might be dead. And the sooner you accept that fact, the faster we can move on to the more important issue."

"More important? What's more important to me than *me* being dead?"

The bird fluttered his wings and lifted off the ground for a second. "Who killed you, of course. That's the more important issue."

Billy felt himself deflate. His body, or whatever it was he was carrying around, slumped forward in sad disappointment. "Someone killed me?" he asked, dejectedly. "Why would someone kill me?"

"That's what we're here to find out. That's the whole point of the exercise. You were murdered, Billy." The bird flew up and landed on a power line. "So get up off the road."

"Why? Why should I get up off the road after hearing that news?"

The bird lifted its shoulder in what could only be described as a shrug. "Because you're about to get hit by a truck. And if you don't think you're dead now, you are going to be pretty soon."

Six

Dale Ghostkeeper loved his Ford truck. It was a fully loaded F-150, diamond blue, with a black interior and heated, leather bucket seats. The in-dash media interface had DVD/CD/MP3 capability with twelve speakers, which included two subwoofers. The truck even had power-heated tow mirrors, a spray-in bed liner and a $2200 lariat chrome and off-road package, even though he never towed anything, never hauled anything in the box and the only off-road driving he ever did was when he cruised the gravel roads of the Rez.

But it was the kind of truck a dude like him needed. It was hard and tough on the outside, ready for anything a gangsta should need, although the only gangsta Dale knew were the rappers he heard on his stereo. The truck was also cool, so he could connect with the ladies. So far the only member of the female persuasion that had ever ridden in his truck was his Aunt Kena.

And that was where he was heading: Aunt Kena's house. He made a weekly trip to her home, loading up her fridge and kitchen with food and other stuff she needed. But the main reason he went to her place was to make sure the crazy old lady was still alive. Aunt Kena lived alone in her little house at the edge of the Rez. It was a creepy old house surrounded by trees, but all of them were dead. There was no grass to speak of, no plants except for a few dead juniper bushes flanking the front steps.

Every time he came within a hundred feet of the place, he swore he could feel a noticeable drop in temperature, even on the hottest and sunniest day. And the regular sounds of the outdoors—the wind, birds, a jet flying overhead—seemed to disappear as soon as he stepped between the dead juniper bushes.

Everyone told him his Aunt Kena could talk to the spirit world, speak to those who had crossed over to the other side. Dale wasn't into that old Native mystical stuff; he really thought his aunt was just a crazy old bird. But her place still gave him the creeps. He never wanted to bring stuff to her every week, but that was the deal he had made with his mom. It had been her duty to check on the old woman, but his mom had passed it on to him. He didn't need his mom's help to make the down payment on his truck; he had a pretty sweet job in the city, working IT for a medium-sized computer company. All he had to do was to sit at his computer and keep an eye on things. Nothing major ever happened except for the odd harddrive crash or forgotten password.

So Dale had the money for the down payment. But he was a young male member of a First Nations band. So even though he had a decent job, no bank was going to give him a loan. Hence the need for his mom to co-sign. And his new weekly duty of making sure crazy Aunt Kena was still alive.

He was about a mile from his aunt's house, rolling over the gravel road, with Marshall Mathers blasting through the subwoofers. The sun was high and bright, creating a glare on the windshield. And for a second, Dale thought he saw a man sitting in the middle of the road about fifty yards ahead.

It wasn't unusual for someone to walk on the side of the road; a lot of folks on the Rez didn't have vehicles, and if they did, most of them didn't work. But *sitting* in the road was something different. And in front of the guy in the road was some kind of bird.

Dale hit the horn of his truck, but the guy didn't move. So he slammed on his brakes. The ABS brakes kicked in, but with the loose gravel, the tires couldn't grab hard enough.

"Holy shit!" Dale shouted, gripping the steering wheel tightly and twisting it in order to avoid hitting the man. But that only locked the wheels, and the truck began to skid. "Get out of the way!" Dale yelled, but the guy didn't move and neither did the bird. Dale slammed both his feet against the brake pedal as hard as he could, but he couldn't stop the forward momentum of the truck.

He was going to run over the guy in the middle of the road.

A second before he did, he realized the man looked a lot like his cousin Billy.

Seven

Billy saw the truck coming and knew he should get out of the way, but he froze. He was like a deer caught in the headlights, mesmerized by the daytime running lights and the stylized white Ford logo on a blue background. The logo reminded him of the commercials during hockey games on TV that he used to watch when he was a kid.

Time appeared to slow down, and Billy watched as the truck locked into a four-wheel skid, the tires scraping against the gravel and raising a cloud of dust that seemed to rise in slow motion. He counted the ridges of the front grill as the truck bore down on him.

Billy looked up and spotted the frightened look on the driver's face. He recognized the driver. It was Dale, his younger cousin. Dale's eyes were wide, his mouth open in a silent scream, his knuckles white as he tightly gripped the steering wheel. Dale was almost standing in his seat, putting all of his substantial weight on the brakes.

Billy smiled for a second, seeing Dale as he was now, a wannabe gangsta with his oversized ball cap cocked sideways and a gray zip-up hoodie with a Detroit Pistons basketball jersey underneath. But Billy remembered Dale in another way.

Almost fifteen years ago, Billy was a tough high school kid, ready to drop out to join one of the gangs on the Rez because that's where all the excitement was. Dale was entering grade seven, barely twelve years old, had yet to shed his baby fat and was always keen on fitting in.

He wore jeans torn at the knees, a loose-fitting green cardigan over a white T-shirt on which he himself had written *Corporate Magazines Still Suck* in black marker. It was the exact look Kurt Cobain had on the cover of *Rolling Stone* in 1992 when Nirvana was big. Dale's hair wasn't as long as Cobain's, but he had mussed it up to look shaggy, and he sported a pair of dark sunglasses and a resigned swagger.

Dale was trying to adjust to his new school for grades seven to twelve, but he was trying too hard. Although some kids still listened to Nirvana and thought the band was still kind of cool, Kurt Cobain had been dead for a few years. So Dale's attempt to be cool was dated, the same way his present attempt to be cool by dressing like Eminem was also dated.

Billy had found Dale's Nirvana image quite funny, but he said nothing. To do so would attract the kid's attention, and Billy didn't want anybody to know that he was related to this loser.

But Dale stuck with his grunge slacker image, and as he walked by Billy and his friends in the school hallway, he gave a quick glance in Billy's direction and just offered a slight nod of his head. If you weren't looking, you wouldn't have noticed it.

Billy had to admit that it was a pretty cool move; Billy's gang of friends was the toughest in the school, a couple were already members of a local gang. So for Dale not to have run up to Billy and demand that they hang out but instead offer a disinterested slacker nod as a means of acknowledgment was pretty damn smart.

He returned the nod, only slightly though, so that no one else would notice.

Billy hoped that no one in his gang would notice Dale, but they couldn't help it. They were alpha wannabes packaged in confused teenage hormones. They had to cut down the weak in order to retain their status in the gang.

"Hey, punk," yelled Gar, the leader of their group. Gar wasn't even enrolled in the school; he had been expelled for a wide variety of infractions, including assault on another student and threatening to assault the math/phys-ed teacher.

But Gar was one of the recruiters for the gang, and one of the best places for the gang to recruit new members was from within the school. Most of the teachers and the administrators were just going through the motions at the school and didn't care that most of the students were failing or dropping out. They didn't care that guys like Gar still hung out at the school, as long as they didn't carry any weapons or cause trouble.

The fact of the matter was that during the summer months, Billy had been deemed an official prospect of Gar's gang, and if he did what he was told and helped out the gang, within a year he would get his colors. Which meant he would be allowed to get a tattoo of the gang's symbol on his body and become an official member.

Dale, still in his slacker mode, paused as if he wasn't sure he had heard his name being called. Or if the shout was for him. "Hey, grunge punk, I'm talking to you!" Gar shouted again.

Dale turned around slowly and looked at Gar and pointed at himself.

"Yeah, you, punk," Gar said, gesturing with his index finger. "Come here."

Dale shrugged and slowly moved toward Gar, Billy and the rest of the gang. A sense of dread came over Billy as Dale sauntered over. Despite his look, Dale was a bit of a loser, a naïve kid who thought everyone liked him and thought he was cool, even though most of the kids made fun of him behind his back. He could be smart at times, but mostly he just didn't get how the world worked, even in the tough world of school.

"Yeah, come on. I wanna talk to you," Gar said. His tone seemed friendly, but with an edge to it. Billy knew that Gar was going to do something to Dale. He hoped it would be relatively painless, a quick lesson on who you can or can't trust in the school. But not severe enough that Billy would feel the need to step in and save the kid.

Dale stepped right up to the gang, his shoulders slumped and his head cocked sideways in a classic grunge pose. Billy expected Dale to say something stupid like, "Here I am; now entertain me."

Fortunately, Dale didn't say that. He just stood there, looking disinterested, but Billy knew his cousin was bursting with excitement because Gar and the gang had noticed him. Dale seemed to think he was being called over as a first step into acceptance into their popular clique. But Billy knew the opposite was about to happen.

Billy tensed and waited, hoping for his sake—and Dale's, he realized—that the encounter would end quickly.

"I take it you're a fan of Nirvana," Gar said. "Awesome band, am I right?"

Dale nodded, still saying nothing but obviously itching to break out of character.

"What's your favorite song?"

Dale shrugged. "They're all good."

"Well, duh. Everybody knows that," Gar said, placing his hand on Dale's shoulder. "But someone like you has to have a favorite song. And it better not be 'Teen Spirit' 'cuz that's too easy."

Dale paused for a second, sensing something was about to happen, but he didn't have the sense to realize it would be something bad. "'Polly' is good, I guess."

"Yeah, yeah, 'Polly.' That's a good one," Gar said, humming the tune and singing a couple of words. "That's the song where he's raping her. Totally awesome."

Billy knew that while the song was about the rape of a young girl, it wasn't something to feel totally awesome about. But he said nothing, knowing that contradicting Gar wasn't a good idea.

But Dale didn't know. "Actually, although Cobain wrote the song from the rapist point of view, he didn't do it to glorify rape. That's a common misconception."

Billy winced at the statement, sucking in a quick breath of surprise.

Gar smiled only because it was the opening he was looking for. He was the kind of dude who pushed people to a point where they had to respond to him negatively or stupidly so he could attack. Gar dug his fingers into Dale's shoulder, and the kid grimaced in pain. Gar leaned forward, his face coming within inches from Dale's.

"Are you contradicting me?" Gar said with a growl. "Sounds like this kid is contradicting me." He looked back at his gang with a smile and then roughly shoved Dale backward.

Dale stumbled back several feet across the hallway into a bank of lockers and collapsed onto the floor. His sunglasses fell off his face and onto the floor underneath his leg. The frame snapped with a loud crack, and one of the lenses popped out.

Dale was stunned for a second, and Billy hoped the kid had learned his lesson and stayed down. Instead, Dale saw his broken sunglasses.

"Dammit, you broke my sunglasses," he blurted out. And even as he said it, he realized that he had said the wrong thing.

Time seemed to stop as if all the air was sucked out of the space. Other kids who were watching the spectacle quickly backed away so they wouldn't become collateral damage. A couple of teachers leaned out of their classroom doorways to see what all the ruckus was about but then stepped back and closed the doors. Even Billy felt like walking away; he was conflicted between his loyalty to his gang and his kinship to his younger, weaker cousin. He hoped that Gar would go easy on the kid, but he doubted it.

Gar leapt into action, dashing across the hallway, grabbing Dale by the collar of his shirt and yanking him off the floor. He slammed Dale against the lockers twice, the back of Dale's head hitting the metal with loud clangs.

Gar held Dale up against the locker with one arm, and then with the other, he gave him a full-arm backslap across the face. Dale's nose exploded with blood.

Gar then tossed Dale to the floor and jumped on top of him, straddling his chest and pinning his arms to the ground. Dale groaned, his eyes wide with surprise, fear and pain. Gar reached to his belt and pulled out a knife that was in a sheath. He held the blade in front of Dale's face.

"Nobody talks back to me, you little punk," he hissed, bringing the tip of the knife closer to Dale's nose and sticking it into a nostril. "And you're going to be a lesson to everyone else about doing that."

But Dale wasn't looking at Gar; he glanced over the gang leader's shoulder at his cousin. Billy saw the kid's eyes, full of fear and pain, pleading for his cousin to help him.

Billy shut his eyes and turned away. But he couldn't shut out the image of Dale's face. Billy was only a kid himself, barely seventeen, but he realized that if he walked away from his cousin, it would haunt him for the rest of his life. His gangbanger friends would think it was cool if he allowed Dale to suffer. But his family would never forgive him. They would disown him, call him a traitor to his family and a failed warrior.

In that moment, Billy knew what he had to do.

"Let him go," he said, quietly but firmly.

Gar paused and turned slightly to look at Billy. "What did you say?"

Billy quickly stepped forward, grabbed Gar's neck from behind and yanked him off Dale's chest. Gar's back hit the lockers with a bang.

But unlike Dale, Gar didn't just accept the attack. He jumped up, knife in hand, ready to attack Billy. "Big mistake, Billy. Nobody gets between me and my prey, not even a potential member like you. Step away now, and I might think about forgiving you and still letting you join."

Billy firmly planted his feet to the ground. "Well, nobody picks on my family and gets away with it. Step away now, and I might let you off without a broken arm."

Gar laughed, looking at the other hangers-on for support. Their faces had looks of surprise and confusion.

"You forget, Billy, that I'm the guy with the knife," said Gar as he lunged forward.

Billy stepped back, pulling his body away from the knife. But instinctively, his right hand reached out and grabbed the blade, the sharp edges cutting into the palm of his hand. But he didn't notice the pain. He shifted his body to the side, like Mosum had showed him, and then twisted his arm, pushing it toward Gar.

There was a snapping sound, and Gar screamed in pain. He tried to drop the knife and back away, but Billy didn't let him. He pushed further into Gar, twisting his arm again and bringing the knife hand up higher, with more cracking sounds. Billy shoved Gar against lockers and leaned into him. Their faces were so close their noses almost touched.

Gar's eyes were swimming with shock and pain. But Billy knew he was still conscious. "Nobody messes with my family, Gar. Nobody. You remember that, because if you or any of your stupid gang friends come after me, my cousin or anybody else I know, I'll hunt you down. And I'll hurt you more than you hurt right now."

Billy gave Gar's arm another quick twist. Gar screamed, and then Billy let him go, dropping the gangbanger and his knife to the floor. Billy gave a quick hard look at his former friends and saw the complete fear of him in their eyes. He knew he and Dale were safe from them and anyone else.

He turned to Dale, gently pulled him to his feet and helped him walk to the nurse's office.

The entire scene played in Billy's head even as Dale's truck passed right through his spirit body. He remembered the incident as Dale jumped out of the truck and looked around for the body of the man he'd hit. He remembered his own inner conflict as a teenager. Even though he had been annoyed at Dale for making him lose his chance to join the gang, he was also grateful that Dale helped him lose his chance to join that gang.

He recognized that Dale's appearance on the road wasn't just happenstance, and neither was his appearance at school so many years ago. Billy realized that Dale, with all his foibles and annoying behavior, probably could help him discover the identity of his murderer.

He knew that Dale was on his way to visit Aunt Kena, to bring her supplies and to make sure she was still alive. That was the only reason Dale ever returned to the Rez. And if anyone could help solve Billy's murder, it was his crazy aunt and her supposed ability to commune with the spirit world.

So when Dale laughed out loud and climbed back into his truck to drive away, Billy jumped into the box to go along for the ride to Aunt Kena's.

And as the truck headed back down the gravel road, Billy realized that Gar was still out there, a major leader in the gang now, despite what happened at the school years ago. Billy wondered how long Gar could hold a grudge and whether he had played some role in his death.

Eight

D ale had shut his eyes and waited for the thud of the body against the front of his truck and the bounce of the tires as they crushed the guy under their weight. Dale quickly apologized to any spirit or god who might be listening to him; he promised to sell his truck and stop lying about his life and his accomplishments if they could find some way to avoid killing the guy in the road.

The truck shuddered and then finally came to an abrupt stop, Dale's body jerking forward, held back only by his seatbelt. A cloud of dust enveloped the truck, but Dale kept his eyes shut tight, wishing everything would just go away. He wanted to be back in his basement suite bedroom in the city, safe and warm under his blankets.

The dust wavered and then settled down. The thumping bass and the whiny voice of Marshall Mathers still blared out of the speakers, but the only sound Dale could hear was the hammering of his heart.

His breath came in deep gasps, but somehow he managed to put the truck in park and shut the engine off. Marshall cut out immediately; the sound of the prairie silence seemed to hover over him.

Dale sat in the truck for what seemed like an eternity. He had to climb out eventually and check the damage. But he didn't want to experience the horror of seeing the crushed body on the road.

One time, when he was a kid, his dad ran over a gopher. His dad didn't stop—no self-respecting prairie resident stops when they run over a gopher. If they did get out of their vehicle, it was only to see if the animal was still alive. And if the gopher *was* still alive, they'd get back into their car or truck and back up over the creature once or twice more just to make sure it was dead.

Dale's father had actually laughed when he hit the gopher. He punched his fist in the air and shouted, "Yeah! That's forty-seven for me. A couple weeks and I'll have fifty for the year."

Dale wasn't sure if his father was telling truth; the guy liked to tell stories a lot. Dale knew that everyone who heard the stories knew that they weren't true, probably his father even knew that. But that didn't stop him from telling the stories.

Dale had felt bad for that gopher, and he glanced at the passenger side mirror, hoping his father had missed the gopher.

He hadn't. In the mirror's reflection, Dale saw the gopher flipping and flopping in its macabre death throes. The vision sickened him, causing him to gag and throw up slightly in his mouth. He coughed and then swallowed, feeling the burn of the acid in his throat. Still, he couldn't look away from the mirror, and even though his dad had kept driving at a high speed, Dale could see the gopher. Its writhing slowed, and then it twitched for several seconds until it stopped moving altogether.

The vision of that animal's death never left Dale. Whenever he saw a gopher in the road, he would always slow down or try to swerve to avoid it.

If the sight of a dying gopher in a rearview mirror still had such an effect on his life, Dale knew that the vision of someone crushed under the tires of his truck would haunt him forever. Probably longer.

Dale finally opened his eyes to assess the damage. He didn't see the man. There was nothing on the horizon, nothing in the sky. There were no witnesses to what he had done, and no vehicles were coming toward him from either side of the road.

If he just drove away, he thought, he would be okay. He would not be charged with any sort of crime because no one would ever know he had been here. Someone else would find the body and have to deal with the hassle.

The best part was that he wouldn't have to look at or be haunted by any memories of a dead body.

Dale reached for his keys in the ignition. He pressed his thumb against the key and turned his wrist to start the engine. The engine roared to life, a sound that always sent tingles to Dale's extremities. Marshall Mathers blared from the speakers. Both sounds were so loud and so satisfying to Dale that he almost forgot he had run into someone in the middle of the road. It was like a vision, one of those vivid dreams that seems and feels so real but isn't once you wake up.

Dale hadn't heard or felt any thuds against his truck. He grabbed the gearshift, preparing to shift into drive, knowing he had done nothing wrong because, in reality, nothing had happened. And if it did, it wasn't his fault anyway; the guy was in the middle of the road just asking for it. And there weren't any witnesses either. So he felt safe.

But then he stopped. For a second or two, he held onto the gearshift, part of his mind willing him to put it into drive and get the heck out of there. But then he relaxed his grip and removed his hand. He reached over again, grabbed the ignition key and shut off the engine. The comforting sounds of the engine and the music faded away. The only sound was the wind over the prairie.

Dale sighed. He wasn't a brave man; he was aware of that. Yes, he was a bit of a coward. But he wasn't the kind of guy who would run away from something as serious as this. No matter how horrible the scene was outside his truck, no matter how much trouble he would get into, no matter if the cops did a blood test and discovered traces of marijuana from a hit he'd taken before leaving his place, he would have to face the situation.

Dale removed his sunglasses, slipped off his ball cap and placed them on the passenger seat. He took a deep breath, like a diver before taking a big plunge, opened the door and stepped outside.

He walked to the rear of the truck and steeled himself for the horror and revulsion of the mangled body on the road. He looked.

But he saw nothing.

His heart skipped a beat. He looked up and down the road. Again, nothing. He slowly bent down, grunting with effort, to look underneath the truck, just in case the guy was wedged down there. But he didn't see anything out of the ordinary.

He looked up and down the road again, sure he had missed something. But he saw nothing but gravel.

"The ditch!" he shouted to himself. He started to run toward the ditch to the left of the truck, but after taking a couple of steps, he stopped. Discovering a body was nothing to be excited about. He walked slowly toward the ditch, stretching his neck in order to get a better look but preparing himself for the worst. He shut his eyes for a moment but then realized that was stupid so he opened them again. If he tripped and fell into the ditch, he could fall onto the body, like some character in a horror movie. And that would be an even worse memory to have than seeing a mangled corpse.

When he reached the edge of the ditch and looked down, he saw only weeds and grass. Neither was high enough to hide a body. He felt a wave of elation.

He looked over his shoulder and sighed when he saw the ditch on the other side of the road. The wave of elation immediately disappeared.

Reluctantly, like a child going to the principal's office knowing that he did something wrong, Dale walked across the road to the other ditch. He took a deep breath before he looked in.

Again, nothing. No corpse, no display of body parts. Just more weeds and grass.

For a brief moment, Dale was disappointed at finding no body. Because regardless of the horror, it would at least be a story he could tell the guys over beers. And for a second, he actually thought the idea of him falling over the body in the ditch would be cool. It had the makings of a great story, something that he could tell over and over again, not only because it would have been a cool experience, but it also had some humor. But it was a story in which he wasn't entirely bragging; it would show that he was okay with making fun at his own expense. So he could tell it again and again without looking like a total idiot with an overblown sense of himself.

But then he snapped back to reality and felt relieved. And a bit stupid. There had been no man on the road, only a trick of the sunlight brought on by the angle of the sun and the THC in the marijuana he had smoked about an hour or so earlier.

Dale began to laugh, first a bit of a giggle and then big guffaws that shook his whole body. It was a mirage, he thought. A trick of light. Now *that* was a story he could tell the guys over beers: I was so stoned that I thought I ran over a guy sitting in the middle of the road. He would recall all the bits about his panic, him checking under the truck and looking in the ditches. He would start the story as if he had actually hit someone and then finish it with a big joke on himself. He could pass himself off as a hero buffoon because, though he was stoned and didn't really hit anyone, he did get out of his truck to check. He didn't run away.

Dale laughed again and headed to his truck so he could finish his errand of taking stuff to Aunt Kena's house. He climbed in and started the engine. But before he drove away, he powered down the driver's window. He stuck his head out, looking down the road ahead of him and then behind, paranoia taking over.

There was nothing. Except for a crow sitting on a power line above the road. The vision of the bird sent a shiver through Dale because in his vision, a crow had been standing next to the guy in the road. But he shook off the image. There was no body, no guy in the road. The crow might have been real, but the guy wasn't.

The crow looked down at Dale and squawked once. Dale sensed that it was best he get as far away from this bird as possible.

So he powered up the window, put the truck in gear and roared away.

As he did, he heard a small thud in the box of his truck, but he figured it was only a rock or something that had fallen in.

He decided that for the next couple of hours, he was going to avoid checking his rearview mirror.

Nine

Billy sat in the box of the truck as it drove down the gravel road. His body felt tired and sore, and he wondered why. He was apparently dead; he had sort of accepted that now. But if he was dead, why was he sore? Why did his head still hurt? How come he had to travel in the back of Dale's truck?

And most importantly, who had murdered him? And why?

Billy racked his brain, trying to piece together the events that led to his death. But the only thing he recalled was a bright flash, no doubt the shot that had killed him. And then nothing. Except waking up in the ravine with an annoying crow screeching at him.

The crow sat in the back of the truck as well, below the rear window, out of the wind, near Billy's left thigh. The bird's eyes were closed and his breathing was even. Every few seconds, a soft whistle would emanate from him, almost as if the crow was snoring.

Crows were relatively large birds, at least compared to the little sparrows and chickadees that ate the seeds from Billy's backyard bird feeder, but seated next to Billy, this crow seemed tiny, almost pet-like. For some reason he couldn't fathom, Billy felt like patting the bird.

He gingerly reached out his hand. But just before he could touch the top of the bird's head, the crow jerked awake, spotting Billy's hand above his head. The bird jumped away, screeching and then snapping his beak forward to peck at Billy's hand. Billy snatched his hand away, even though he knew he was dead, and theoretically, the bird couldn't hurt him.

"What the heck are you doing?" the crow yelled. "Trying to kill me or something?"

Billy gave the bird a shocked look. "No, I wasn't trying to kill you. Why would I want to kill you? I'm dead anyway so I don't really think I could kill you if I wanted to. Could I?"

"No, you couldn't kill me. But what's the deal with the hand? What were you doing?"

"I was going to…," Billy paused, realizing that trying to pet the crow was a silly idea. And even more silly was saying that out loud to a talking bird. "Uh, never mind. Just forget it."

The bird leaned forward and looked up at Billy. "Were you going to pet me?" he asked with an incredulous tone.

Billy shook his head wildly and waved his hands. "No, I wasn't going to pet you. Why would I want to pet you?" Billy could feel his face flushing; he was a terrible liar.

"You were," the bird said with a bit of a laugh. "You were going to pet me."

"No, I wasn't."

"Yes, you were. You were going to pet me. That's rich."

Billy sighed, wondering how much worse this day could get. First he had woken up in a ravine, thinking he had fallen off the wagon after thirteen years of sobriety. But then he had found out he was dead. Murdered. Shot in the head. And to top it all off, he couldn't go into the afterlife, or wherever people went when they died; he was stuck in the back of a pickup truck, going god knows where. And to make matters even worse, a talking crow was making fun of him.

"Big deal. So I was going to pet you. You looked kind of cute sitting there asleep."

The bird shook his head in dismay. "Man, you're going to owe me *big* after this one, bear," he mumbled to himself.

"What?" Billy asked, unable to make out the bird's words.

The crow shook his head again, bringing himself back to the present. He hopped toward Billy, raising a wing in the air. "Listen, Billy. I don't like this any better than you do. If I had my druthers, or even knew what the heck druthers were in the first place, I'd be somewhere else, preferably near a landfill site or on a tree bugging the heck out of a couple of cats. But I'm not. I'm stuck with you until you figure out who killed you, and why, so you can make amends for the negative things you've done in your life."

"Negative things? What the heck are you talking about? What negative things? I was a good guy."

"Well, if you were a such good guy, a good and honorable Native warrior, then you'd be in the Happy Hunting grounds with all the other good and honorable Native warriors, wouldn't you? But you're not. So you must have done something wrong, something pretty serious because you don't get stuck behind like this for not paying your parking tickets."

Billy thought for a moment, trying to figure out what bad stuff he had done in his life. Sure, there was the drinking, but he had done the twelve steps, made amends and all that, *and* stayed sober for thirteen years. That had to count for something. He paid his taxes on time, didn't try to beat the system even though he could have, with his treaty card. And he did his job with relative honesty and efficiency. It wasn't easy being the band compliance officer and making sure the oil, timber and mining companies fulfilled their commitments, be they financial, environmental or employment-wise. Sure, he had looked the other way a few times with the natural gas drilling and with some of the emission controls, and he received a few gifts from the corporation because of it. But everyone did that. It was just part of doing business, and even the chief and band council encouraged this behavior to ensure royalties and jobs flowed into the Rez at a smooth rate.

No harm was done in the long run, Billy thought.

Just at that moment, the truck hit a bump, and the pain in Billy's head exploded. He fell back against the truck box, a massive light searing his brain.

"...and whatever you do," the crow continued, "you will never try to pat me again because I am not a pet; I am a spirit guide and deserve respect...." The bird paused when he noticed Billy had fallen against the truck, stricken with pain.

The crow hopped onto Billy's knee and looked deeply into his eyes. "Ho, boy, you are carrying a lot of dark baggage, my friend. You must have done something terribly wrong."

Ten

By the time Billy regained his senses, Dale's truck had pulled up outside Aunt Kena's house. Dale stepped out of the truck and spun around as if he was facing an army of invisible ninjas, and then after a second, dashed between the dead juniper bushes and clambered up the decaying front steps. He banged on the screen door and yanked on the door handle at the same time. The door was locked, but Dale vigorously shook the handle, causing the glass in the screen door to rattle. He looked about wildly, his eyes wide with fear, and his breathing came in gasps, like someone running from a mob of zombies or a serial killer armed with a chainsaw.

He shook the door handle again. "Come on, Auntie, open up. Open up!" And he banged harder.

He looked around the yard, and just as he did, Aunt Kena arrived at the door and silently pushed it open. Feeling the door move behind him, Dale turned and yelped like a little girl frightened by a ferocious dog and jumped straight up into the air.

His reaction caused Aunt Kena to yank the door closed with a loud metal clang, and she screamed in response. The violent sound and movement of the door, along with his aunt's screaming, caused Dale to yell again because he thought she was either a zombie or some other evil being. He tried to yank open the door again, but it wouldn't budge.

The experience of hitting a guy in the middle of the road and then discovering that the man had disappeared, or that he had only imagined the whole thing, along with the sound he heard from the back of his truck, had all completely unnerved him.

Dale had a sense that something or someone was following him, and he had no idea who or what it was. He remembered stories of the Wendigo, the legendary Cree monster that would torment and follow its victims for weeks, sometimes even months, in order to drive them crazy with fear until finally, they would give themselves up to the Wendigo. And though he was a tough Native bro with the most amazing truck ever and had loads of chicks waiting for him in the city, Dale still believed in such entities as the Wendigo. And that his Auntie Kena had the Eyes of Fire. Those he saw firsthand every week.

But what worried him the most was not that the Wendigo would get him, but that he would turn out like his auntie and live alone in a pathetic little house at the edge of the Rez with no one to visit but a lone nephew and nothing in her life but her TV and those spirits that she claimed to talk to. Of course, Dale didn't make the connection between his auntie's solitary life and his own life of living alone in a small one bedroom apartment at the edge of downtown with no one to visit him, not even an aunt or a nephew. He had nothing in his life except for his X-Box and the pretend conversations he had with various hip-hop celebrities, practice for when he became a famous MC.

"What the heck is wrong with you, Eyikos?" Kena demanded angrily. Even though Dale was scared out of his mind, he cringed at the sound of that nickname. Only Aunt Kena called him that, Eyikos, which in Cree meant "little ant." When he was a kid, he liked the name because ants were the most numerous creatures in the world. And they could lift ten times their weight. But as he got older, ants began to represent smallness, something that could be crushed under a boot.

"You should just go home, Eyikos," Kena continued to yell. "Even though you almost scared me half to death with your shouting and screaming, you at least know that I'm still alive, that I haven't died in the past week. And I don't need any new groceries because I still got almost half of the stuff you brought me last week. I don't eat as much as you guys think I do."

Dale reached out for the door, again trying to open it, but Kena grabbed it at the same time, keeping it shut.

When elders scolded Dale, he had no idea what to say to them. Even if he knew he wasn't in the wrong, or if there was a good reason for his actions, such as being stalked by a Wendigo, he became tongue-tied and confused.

So the only way he could respond to his aunt was to step back, look at his shoes and offer a heavily mumbled, "Sorry."

"Is that all you got to say for yourself, Dale Ghost-keeper? Do you think *sorry* is enough for almost killing your auntie? You seem to always talk tough, but when it really comes down to it, to the important stuff, the only thing you can muster is *sorry*?"

"Please, Aunt Kena," Dale said, looking over his shoulder and expecting something to jump out at him at that very instant. "You gotta let me in."

"I don't have to do anything you…" Aunt Kena started to say. But then she looked past Dale and saw what was behind him. She gasped once. Her expression changed from angry to one of terrible sadness and disappointment. Along with those feelings was a dreadful fear of what that sadness had brought with it.

She flung the door open and grabbed her nephew's arm and pulled him in. The power of her strength threw Dale across the room. He stumbled and fell against the couch. Aunt Kena slammed shut the screen door. She locked it and then hooked the chain that Dale had installed months earlier. She pressed her back against the door, her massive frame providing even more security.

Dale looked up at her, and the look of fear on her face only deepened the fear inside of him.

"Eyikos," she hissed at him. "What the hell did you do?"

Eleven

Billy had jumped out of the truck and was heading toward Aunt Kena's door. But when he saw Dale freaking out, he stopped.

Can Dale see me? he wondered. If Dale could, that was a bit of good news. Billy knew that Aunt Kena could probably help him somehow, but in the last few years after her hip injury, she barely left the house. She might have been able to give him advice about his new situation—that is, if she could see him—but she probably couldn't offer any practical assistance.

The possibility of Dale being aware of his presence offered Billy a little hope. Despite Dale's shortcomings, he was at least mobile and was relatively willing to interact with people in the real world.

Billy moved toward the front door of the house, but as he did, he saw a look of fear come over his aunt's face. Billy froze for a second, thinking he was the source of her fear.

But she wasn't looking at him. She was looking above and behind him, at something in the sky.

Billy turned and saw the crow perched on the power wire. And the look on the crow's face was also a surprise to Billy. It matched the same look on Aunt Kena's: fear.

"What the heck is up with you?" Billy asked the crow.

"Where the heck have you taken me?" the bird said, his body and voice shaking with fear. "What is this place?"

Billy turned and casually pointed at the house. "This place?" he said, confused. "It's just my Aunt Kena's house. She's going to help me figure out who killed me and why."

"You mean you can't see it?" the bird said in a shocked voice. "You can't see what this place is?"

Billy turned and looked at the old house, the paint peeling off the siding, the spots on the roof where shingles were missing and the dead trees, plants and grass surrounding the house. "Looks the same to me," he said. "Hasn't changed in years, although I always wondered why the plants are only barely alive. That's the only thing I can think of."

"You haven't accepted the fact you have died if you can't see what this place really is," the bird shouted at him. "This isn't a simple house. This is a place of great and dangerous power. I would highly recommend that you not go into that house."

Billy looked at the house again, this time squinting to try to see what the heck the bird was talking about. Although the air seemed to shimmer a bit, nothing else had changed.

"I have to go in there. Aunt Kena is the only person who can help me. She has the Eyes of Fire."

"The Eyes of Fire!" the crow exclaimed in horror. "She has a lot more than the Eyes of Fire! That is one dangerous auntie you are dealing with. Even your Mosum the bear would be afraid of her."

"Are you kidding? It's only Aunt Kena," Billy said. "She's a little crazy, talks to herself all the time, and they said she used to be a pretty good healer, but she's harmless."

"Harmless? There's nothing harmless about this place and the creature that dwells in it. Take my advice, Billy. Turn around and walk away. We'll figure this thing out another way. I don't care if it takes forever, anything is better for you than going into that place."

"I don't want to walk around forever trying to figure this thing out. I want to figure it out soon and get on with whatever I'm supposed to get the heck on with now that I'm dead," Billy said angrily. "And if that means going into Aunt Kena's house and discovering she's some kind of zombie monster that eats the souls of dead people, that's what I gotta do."

"A zombie monster that eats the souls of dead people is something I can handle, but this…" said the crow, pointing at the house with his right wing, "…this is beyond my control. It's something beyond anybody's control."

Billy looked at the house again, still seeing nothing but an old Rez house owned by a crazy old lady who talked to herself. When he was a kid, everyone used to say Aunt Kena was crazy, that she had the Eyes of Fire and that people should stay away from her, but she had always been nice to him. On the few occasions he did see her, either during a visit or at a powwow, at least when she used to go out, she always recognized him, calling him by name. And unlike some of his other older relatives, Aunt Kena never tried to hug him or drown him in slobbery kisses. She only gently touched his left ear lobe with the tip of her index finger and then quietly, like a magician doing slight-of-hand magic, she'd place a little piece of candy or chocolate in his hand. And her candies and chocolates were always the ones that kids liked, not the funny-tasting kinds that the other older relatives would try to pass off as "sweets."

Billy also remembered the stories that said Aunt Kena could talk to the spirit world. So she was probably the only person who could help him, now that he was in the spirit world. Or trapped somewhere between the real world and the spirit one.

And given the way Dale had reacted at their aunt's front door, Billy was sure his cousin could help somehow. Regardless of what the crow said, Billy had to go into the house and ask his aunt for help. And that's what he told the crow.

"It's your funeral," the crow said without any irony in his voice.

"There's nothing she can do to hurt me now that I'm dead."

The crow snorted. "Don't be so sure about that. Just because you're dead doesn't mean you still can't be hurt in another way. I'm a spirit guide with all the powers that go with the office, and I'm still leery and fearful of many things. Whatever is in that place falls on the extreme spectrum of the fear meter."

"Well, I'm not afraid. It's only Aunt Kena. She's a decent person."

"Are you sure about that? Family members usually cause the greatest harm."

"Regardless, I'm going in," Billy said with a shrug. "You coming with me?"

The bird shook his head vigorously. "Nothing could make me go in there. Not even the end of all life."

"Then I'll have to go in without you."

"Good luck," the bird said.

Billy started walking toward the door, though with some minor trepidation because of the crow's reaction. But nothing was going to stop him; he had to talk to Aunt Kena.

When Billy was within a few feet of the front steps, the bird called out in a quiet voice. "Billy."

Billy stopped, but he didn't turn around. He looked over his shoulder, and in his peripheral vision he saw the crow still perched on the wire. "What?" Billy asked.

"If you are set in your mind on going in there, be warned you may learn something that could harm you. Not physically but in other ways. You may consider her to be your Aunt Kena, and there's a good chance she probably is, but people shouldn't learn certain things about themselves and what they've done in their past. If you walk through

that door and talk to that powerful creature, you will probably learn of these things, and if you're not strong enough, it
could destroy you."

"I'm already dead," Billy said, plainly. "How much
worse could it get?"

Billy turned his head forward and continued to walk
to the house and up the front steps. He opened the door and
walked in.

"Oh, it can get a lot worse than dead," the crow whispered, as he watched Billy disappear through the door.

Twelve

The first thing that hit Billy when he walked into the house was the smell. It was an unpleasant but not overpowering stink of sweat, mildew and something else that smelled like someone had burnt bannock several days ago but forgot to open the window.

The only light in the room was coming from the TV in the living room just off to the right of the front entrance hallway. He stepped in farther, looking around the living room.

The sound of the TV was muted, and the actors on the screen looked even crazier when they were silently screaming at each other. Kind of like the silent slapstick of the Keystone Cops mixed with a Bugs Bunny cartoon.

Billy glanced away from the TV and looked around the room. It had been years since he had visited his aunt, but nothing in the room had changed. The old Lazy Boy recliner was still against the left wall, its light-brown faux leather cracked and peeling. Next to it was an end table covered with a gray doily. A glass containing some kind of brownish liquid sat abandoned on the table.

Across from the recliner was a long, wide sofa, missing a leg on the front left side, causing it to lean forward. It was covered with an old Hudson Bay blanket. Billy remembered the blanket from when he was a kid, and it was old and scratchy even then, twenty years ago. Back then, he had sat down on the same couch with the same blanket and he had gotten sick. It had been a horrible illness that lasted a long time, most of it he could barely remember, save for competing bouts of bone-shivering chills and sauna-level heats. And the sound of his Aunt Kena's voice droning, seemingly forever, a Cree song that struck him deep in his soul. Someone had made him drink a foul-tasting liquid that tasted like bark rolled in dirt and then boiled in bacon fat.

After recovering from his illness, Billy recalled that he rarely got sick again as a kid, except for the odd cold that barely produced a case of the sniffles. He thought it was unusual he could remember all these small details about his life growing up but couldn't recall what had happened to him in the last few days before his death.

A scuffling sound down the hall interrupted his thoughts. He moved farther into the house, into the area where the hallway intersected. One direction led to the kitchen—every inch of the counter was covered with dirty plates, glasses and dried herbs. In the other direction were the bedrooms and bathroom.

The door to bathroom was open, but a reek that Billy didn't want to think about nor dissect in his mind hung around the entrance. He walked quickly down the hall.

At the end of the hall were three bedrooms, two of which had their doors open. He saw a large variety of planters filled with seemingly dead plants, herbs hanging from the ceiling and rows upon rows of jingle dance cones of various sizes. The metal cones bumped against each other, as if a permanent breeze blew in the room, creating a welcoming hum of jingling. Underneath that sound Billy thought he heard the sounds of a powwow, the drums and the voices distant, barely audible.

The third bedroom door was closed, but Billy heard scuffling behind the door. He grabbed the doorknob with his right hand but the knob was hot—not enough to burn but hot enough to make him jump and pull his hand away.

Billy grabbed the handle again and reminded himself he was dead and couldn't feel heat or be burned. The instant the thought came into his head, the heat disappeared. He turned the handle and opened the door.

He saw someone large hiding on the floor, behind the bed, moaning. The person wore an oversized ball cap so Billy figured it was Dale. Aunt Kena, though, was sitting at the foot of her bed, her back erect, as if she was at some treaty signing.

She was wearing a faded red dress that would have reached the floor on any other woman, but because of Aunt Kena's immense body, the hem of the dress only came to the top of her knees. Her brown bare legs were fleshy and fat, the skin rippling. She wore her hair in two long braids that hung over her chest.

Billy knew she was an old woman—she had been old when he was a kid—and though her face was wrinkled and her hair was mostly gray, there was something about her, a glow of some sort, that made her seem a lot younger than he remembered.

"Who's there?" his aunt asked, her voice crackling with age but strong and demanding. She looked at him, but at the same time, not at him. Her eyes were focused in his direction but she didn't look him in the eye.

"It's me, Aunt Kena," Billy said.

Her eyes seemed to focus on his movements, and for a brief moment she made eye contact with him. Her look sent a shock through Billy, not a painful shock, but just like being hit with a strong gust of wind. Billy staggered backward.

Aunt Kena frowned, as if she didn't recognize him. "I asked who's there," she said again, sending another shock his way.

Billy waited till it flowed through him, this time allowing the power to become part of him instead of fighting it. "It's me, Aunt Kena. Your nephew Billy."

It took a second, but she smiled as she connected with his eyes and recognized the man standing at her bedroom door. "Billy," she said softly. "Oh, Miss Pîyesî," she added, her Cree nickname for him. Billy knew that it meant "large bird," which he figured was an eagle or something.

And then her face fell into sadness and disappointment. Tears appeared in her eyes as she gave him a sorrowful look. Her shoulders slumped, and she looked as if she had aged thirty years in that one second. "Oh Billy, Billy, Billy," she whispered. "Oh, Miss Pîyesî. Look what happened to you."

Billy stared at his auntie, feeling a wave of sadness come over him. For the first time since he had discovered he was dead, he actually felt like he was dead. Even though he was still roaming as a spirit, he would do no more in this world. He was done, complete, but at the same time incomplete because when he looked back on his life, on what he could remember, he saw no major events. There were moments of love and some minor accomplishments, such as finishing high school and not joining the gang, but that was nothing really. For Native youth, maybe finishing high school counted as a major accomplishment, but for other kids in the rest of the country, it was typical. Almost every kid finished high school; no big deal.

Billy had never married, never had kids, never moved past anything besides his own personality and needs. His life had been a waste, he thought. Even Dale, with all his faults, had accomplished more than Billy, not just completing high school but earning a two-year diploma from a community college. Dale had a job in the city, writing code for some computer company, and he even stayed connected to his home by driving to the Rez every week to take care of their aunt.

Billy felt as though he was going to melt with sadness and regret, but Aunt Kena suddenly jumped back to life, her spine snapping up straight. She clapped her hands once. The sound cracked the air like a sonic boom, rattling the entire house.

"Billy!" she shouted at him. He looked at her, and her face was angry and determined. "Don't you know you're supposed to knock and ask permission before you enter a house?"

Billy looked at his aunt, confused. He thought about the movies and TV shows he had seen about the dead and the undead, vampires and zombies. "Is that rule because I'm dead? I'm not allowed to enter a house unless I receive permission from the resident?"

Aunt Kena laughed, a big rolling sound. "No, you idiot. You should always knock first and ask permission before entering someone's home because that's what polite people do," she said with a smile. "I know your Mosum taught you better than that after your mother passed."

"Oh, yeah. Sorry," Billy said sheepishly.

"That's okay. You're confused because you're dead. Happens all the time."

"So what do I do now?"

"Why are you asking me?" she said. "You're the one who came here."

"Right, I guess I need your help."

"To do what? To find your way to the spirit world?"

"I guess."

"That's easy. Just start walking and it will find you."

"But I can't do that. I was told I had to stay and figure things out."

"Yes, I've seen the creature you are traveling with," Aunt Kena said with frown. "Don't listen to him, Miss Pîyesî. He's a powerful and dangerous creature who can't be trusted."

Billy grunted. "Actually, the crow said the same thing about you."

"He would. He's also very cunning."

"He says Mosum sent him."

"Mosum did. That's the kind of guy he is. Sending someone else to do his dirty work."

"But can you help me?"

"Help you do what?"

"I don't know. Help me figure out who murdered me and why?"

Aunt Kena's eyes narrowed. She stared at Billy for a brief while. And then she shook her head.

"No," she said plainly. "I won't help you."

"What!" Billy said, incredulous. "What do you mean you won't help me? I'm your nephew. You have to help me."

Aunt Kena stood up from her bed, and the whole house began to shake. She seemed to grow in height, and the ceiling above her turned black, they way the sky did before a severe thunderstorm.

"I do not have to help you, Billy Ghostkeeper. You are nothing but Miss Pîyesî."

"Yeah, an eagle. What's wrong with eagles? Eagles are great."

"Eagle? 'Miss Pîyesî' doesn't mean 'eagle.' It means 'big bird.'"

"Yeah, like an eagle."

"No, like that big yellow bird on TV. Always stomping around, full of promise but always getting things wrong. You lost your way as a human being and turned your back on your people. Your actions have caused great harm, so if you have to walk the earth as a spirit for the rest of eternity, then you deserve what you get."

Before Billy could respond, his aunt flicked her fingers at him, producing an explosion of light. The bright light blinded Billy, and when it finally subsided, he found himself outside Aunt Kena's house at her front door.

He grabbed the screen door and tried to open it. It was locked.

"Told you," the crow said from behind Billy.

"Shut up,' Billy said, pulling the door handle again. But it wouldn't open.

He looked through the screen, ready to shout angrily to be allowed in. But through the screen he could see two faces. Two children, a boy about ten and a girl about six, stared back at him, their faces sad, yet resigned. They said nothing to him, only blinking a couple of times. He stared at the kids, knowing they looked familiar, but he couldn't place them.

Another flash of light came from within the house, and in that instant Billy recognized the kids. He knew their names, knew their parents, knew why they were at Aunt Kena's house—they were spirits, just like him. And the worst part was that he knew their deaths were all his fault. They were dead because of him. Because of something he did. Or rather, didn't do.

He fell to his knees and wept.

Thirteen

Billy had loved his new job. He was only a couple years out of high school and already he was pulling down forty thousand dollars a year as the assistant compliance officer for the band.

And the job wasn't hard. All he had to do was drive around the Rez and various parts of the Crown land that was classified as traditional land and stick meters into the air near some wells to measure air quality, dig up bits of dirt here and there or get water samples from the rivers, streams and creeks in the area.

And then he had to take all the samples to the lab at the band office, run it through the machines and then write down the numbers. If he found problems with the numbers, he had to notify his supervisor, Matt.

Matt was a likeable and cheerful Indian. He liked to tell stupid jokes, drink beer and watch sports on TV after work. And best of all, he didn't hassle Billy.

If Billy had to go somewhere during work hours, like run an errand, Matt didn't mind. If Billy was late in getting his samples to the lab, Matt didn't mind that either.

In fact, Matt encouraged Billy to take his time. "The Rez is a big place, Billy. There are a lot of wells out on the land, lots of rivers, lots of air," Matt would say with his big hearty laugh. "So there's no need to rush. Take your time, enjoy the sights."

So Billy did. He drove around when he felt like it, his arm hanging out the truck's window, Metallica playing on the stereo. *Master of Puppets* was an old album but sounded totally awesome when driving the backroads of the Rez in the summer. Life was great.

But it was about eight months into the job when Billy actually started paying attention to the numbers he was gathering. It was a wintery Thursday in January, and he hadn't gone out to get samples in several weeks. During that time he was supposed to be reading up on the new government standards, reading various trade magazines and keeping up his knowledge and skills.

He knew most of the info, but it was dry stuff. In short, he was bored.

So just for kicks, he was in the lab and he clicked on the sampling machines, intent on testing stupid stuff, like his piss, his spit, the air out of a balloon and some poop from the litter box of the office cat. No one discovered what he was doing because no one from the band office ever went to the lab, and Matt was on vacation in Cuba.

But Billy never got to the sampling. When all the machines came on, they reverted to their last test result. Billy looked at all the machines, recalling some of the numbers he had written down when he had first started the job. The new numbers on the machines seemed to be much higher than usual.

Billy first thought something was wrong with the machines so he shut them all down and restarted them. The numbers came up the same.

He had nothing better to do, so he decided to check the data from the last few months. He booted up his computer, opened the files and reviewed the numbers.

As Billy was checking the numbers, he realized that nothing was wrong with the machines; the numbers *were* getting higher. Some of them, especially the air and water samples in certain areas, were at dangerous levels. He made a note of those samples, where they were taken and headed out to check the areas. He had nothing better to do.

It was a cold winter, but Billy was used to driving the snow-covered country roads. He made sure he had his emergency road kit and drove off.

It took him a few days to find and check all the locations. Most of the wells were pretty remote. No one lived nearby, and only a few elders still ran trap lines.

But one or two well sites were located near homes that were several miles away from the village. A group of related families lived in those houses, their well water less than half a mile from a couple of sour well sites. A stream also close to the well sites led into the village's water supply.

When Billy got to the lab, he noted all his findings and wrote up a report the way he was trained to do it. He almost sent the report to the admin office and to the resource company that owned the wells, but he decided to wait until Matt returned from his vacation. He knew Matt would want to see the report, and Billy was willing to let Matt take credit for his work.

Billy figured it was better if the senior officer filed the report.

So when Matt returned to work and Billy showed him the report, the supervisor said nothing for about a minute. Then he laid down the papers on his desk and scratched his head.

"You were busy while I was gone, weren't you?" Matt said with a laugh. But it wasn't his typical guffaw; this laugh was restrained and seemed nervous.

"I was bored out of my mind. I needed to do something with myself, or I'd go crazy."

Matt nodded but didn't seem to be listening. "Did you file this through the proper channels like you were trained to do?" Matt's voice was tense, as if he was angry or something.

"No, man, I'm sorry," Billy said, mentally kicking himself for not following procedure. He hoped Matt wouldn't get angry at him because of it. "I know I was supposed to, but I wanted to run it by you, make sure I did everything right.

And honestly, I was hoping that you would file the report. You could take credit for it if you want; I don't really care. I didn't even print out a copy, just in case."

The tension in Matt's face faded, and soon he was smiling like the old Matt. "It's okay, Billy. As long as you didn't file it or tell anyone about your findings."

"I told no one."

"Good. You leave that report with me, and I'll take care of it, okay?"

"Sure, Matt. Sorry if I kind of surprised you with it. I thought about calling you, but I didn't want to ruin your vacation."

"That's mighty decent of you, but next time, try not to take on too much initiative while I'm gone. There's a reason why I'm the supervisor here."

Billy nodded, feeling somewhat ashamed but still relieved Matt wasn't angry with him.

Matt stood up, walked over to Billy, put a hand on his shoulder and gave him a slight shake. "Get your jacket, Billy. I want to show you something and introduce you to someone."

They put on their jackets and went outside and climbed into Matt's truck. It was a beautiful machine with all the bells and whistles, including heated seats made out of the softest leather Billy had ever felt. While the truck warmed up, Matt pointed at the band office.

"Billy, have you ever thought about how we were able to build such a nice band office?" Matt asked.

Billy looked at the band office, which was a beautiful structure designed to look like a traditional longhouse. He knew his people didn't build longhouses, but the architect thought the idea would work and the band council thought so too. The building also had state-of-the-art heating, electrical and computer systems throughout, with some of the highest Green ratings that a building could get in the country. It had even been featured in a couple of architecture trade magazines.

"It's a beautiful building," Billy said.

"Yeah, it's very beautiful. A credit to our community. But how do you think the band was able to afford to build it?"

"I don't know. Government money, I guess?"

Matt laughed one of his hearty laughs. "I don't think so. The government would never pay for something like this even if they wanted it for themselves. Guess again, Billy."

Billy thought for a moment, but the only place bands usually got money from was the government. It took him a second or two to figure it out. "The oil companies?" he finally said, feeling stupid for not thinking of it earlier. "The band got the money from their royalty payments."

"Bingo," Matt said. "Oil royalties paid for this building. We don't really own the oil and the gas; the government does. But we own the land, or at least we used to own the land—our traditional land, the government calls it. The oil and gas companies pay the band a royalty for every barrel of oil or gigajoule of gas they take out of the ground.

The companies pipe out a crapload of that stuff, which in turn pays us a crapload of money."

Matt put the truck in gear and pulled out of the parking lot. He drove slowly through the village, pointing at various buildings. "Check out the new community center, the aqua center, the powwow grounds, even the school you graduated from. All of those facilities were built with the royalty money that the oil company pays us. Your job, indirectly, comes from them."

Matt drove farther away from the band office and continued to speak as he drove. "Without the royalty money, none of this stuff would be here. This whole place would be empty, and we'd be just another poor reserve with no running water and no facilities to keep our kids from getting into trouble. And I know you were just doing your job, so I'm not mad at you, but if we file that report with the administration, they would have to send it to the government regulators and there would be all kinds of questions. There's a good chance the wells would be shut down, and there would be no more drilling and no more resource exploration. The band would lose the royalty money, and both of us would be out of a job."

"But the numbers are pretty high," Billy said. "I checked them myself several times, and in some of those locations, there are families with young kids living close by. Some of those readings, especially the air and the water ones, are considered toxic. It can't be good for those kids."

Matt laughed. "Readings can vary depending on the season, wind direction and a lot of other variables. You can't panic and think just because some numbers are high that it's going to affect the health of a few kids. There's a lot of air out there, the groundwater's pretty solid, so you can't push the panic button on the basis of one report."

"But I double-checked everything and covered my tracks just like you taught me."

Matt nodded. "I know you did. And don't get me wrong; you did great work. But there's a system in place when this kind of thing occurs. It's an informal system that gets to the heart of the matter much faster, and it works."

They arrived at the spot where the Rez ended and Crown land began, right near a small strip mall that housed the grocery store, a bank, a fast-food joint, a bar and a couple of offices. Matt pulled into the lot, parking the truck in front of the office building. The sign on the door read "DBA Resources."

Matt got out of the truck and headed to the door. Billy followed. Before Matt opened the door, he turned to Billy. "Let me do the talking. I'll introduce you, but I know these guys and they're okay."

Matt got them past the receptionist, some girl who had been a couple of years behind Billy in high school, and they headed to the back offices. At the door marked "GM," Matt knocked and then walked in.

A tall thin man came out from behind the desk to greet Matt with a smile. He had a military haircut and wore horn-rimmed glasses that made him look like Gary Busey when the actor had played Buddy Holly.

"Hey, Matt," the man said, stretching out a hand that Matt shook vigorously. "How was Cuba? Heard the weather was beautiful. Hope you didn't get sunburn?"

Matt laughed. "Red man doesn't get burned. That's only you Caucasian types."

They laughed together like old friends and shared a bit of small talk, and the man gestured for the two of them to sit.

"So who's the kid?" the oil man asked, looking at Billy.

"This is my assistant, Billy Ghostkeeper." Matt turned to Billy. "This is Grant Menson, Billy. He's the oil company's man in town."

"Good to meet you, Billy," Grant said, holding out his hand. Billy reached out to shake his hand, and Grant's grip was quick, but firm. "So what's up?" Grant said, looking at Matt.

"Well, when I was on holidays, Billy showed a bit of initiative and discovered a bunch of new numbers. He thought they were high, so he did some checking and wrote out an official report."

Grant blinked for a second. "Did he file the report?"

"That he did not do."

Grant blinked again, and this time Billy thought he saw a look of relief cross the man's face. "Well, that's good news."

"Yeah," said Matt. "So I thought it would be a good opportunity to introduce Billy to you and explain to him that in order to forgo all that government red tape and craziness from those pencil pushers in the capital, our informal procedure would be to give you the numbers and let you deal with it yourself, cutting out the middleman."

"Excellent idea, Matt," Grant said, turning to Billy. "You see, it would take months or even a year for the government to figure out what the numbers mean. And they would badger you all the time about it, questioning your abilities and even sending their own people out here to double-check. So they wouldn't even get any of this information to us until they were all done, and we would be way behind in being able to do something about it. This way, we get the info directly and take care of it ourselves."

"You see what he's getting at?" Matt asked, looking at Billy.

Billy nodded, but he wasn't sure. He knew there was a protocol so that the government regulators could stay on top of things, but he also knew the process moved really slowly when government folks got involved. Matt was the one who had trained Billy about these protocols, and since his boss was now telling him about the informal arrangement, it couldn't be bad to do it this way.

"So you guys will deal with this. Make sure there's no problem with the air and water."

"Of course," Grant said. "At DBA Resources, we may be an oil and gas company, but we want to make sure we are doing things right. That's why we came up with this strategy, so we can deal with any problems immediately, instead of months down the road."

Billy nodded again, seeing nothing wrong with the logic. Matt handed the report to Grant, and the oilman read it, nodding in places. After he finished, Grant set the papers down and looked at Billy. "That's some good work, Billy. You really showed good initiative and some good attention to detail. I'd love to have someone like you come work for me."

Billy blushed, but shook his head. "Nah, I like working with Matt. He's a good guy."

"He is," Grant said with a laugh. "But there should be some way we can reward your initiative, to show that we appreciate a hardworking Aboriginal man."

Grant leaned back in his chair. "You know, there's a conference down in Houston next month. Some interesting stuff on environmental stewardship, stuff like that. Some of it is pretty dry, but other stuff is pretty cool. And Houston is a heck of a place. These conferences always have some great outside excursions planned so you can deal with the dry stuff. He'd be perfect for it, eh, Matt?"

Matt nodded. "Yeah, I think he would. I bet with a recommendation from you, Grant, we could talk the band into sending Billy."

"Well, we could offer to pay for Billy's travel expenses if the band paid for the conference. How's that?"

"Yeah, I think we can work that out," Matt said, turning to Billy. "What do you think? Wanna go to Houston?"

A month after he met Grant, Billy was on a plane for the first time in his life, flying business class to Houston.

The conference was a week long, and Grant was right, there were a lot of great social programs.

And the next time the numbers from the samples went up slightly, Billy sent the report to Grant. And then a conference Florida came up that was perfect for Billy. And on it went. There were other conferences, more prizes that he won and special gifts from Grant and the company for following the informal protocol.

Billy realized that the numbers never really went down, but nobody got hurt. And the conferences and the other gifts became a regular occurrence. And he got to keep his job, which now paid him seventy thousand dollars with a new truck thrown in every two years.

But a couple of years later, Billy read in the paper that some local kid had died of leukemia. He was ten years old, the article said. The kid's name was Kyle Jennings. There was a photo of Kyle when he was eight, smiling in his hockey gear before the disease struck. Coincidently, a few months later, Kyle's grandfather died of some rare form of cancer that had never been diagnosed in the province before.

And then about a year after the first death, the paper published the photo of a girl, about six, who also died of leukemia, a shocking yet unforeseen coincidence, an act of God that no one could control. Her name was Susan Jennings, the sister of the boy who had died. Billy also heard that their mother had contracted breast cancer.

Billy decided to check the numbers before the time he had that first meeting with Grant. He discovered that the Jennings family lived in the house where he registered those original toxic readings.

Fourteen

Outside his aunt's house, Billy wept because the two faces that looked out at him were Kyle Jennings and his sister Susan, the two kids who had died of leukemia not so long ago. He realized in that moment it was his fault they had died.

"Tough business, isn't it?" the crow said. "Realizing that because of your actions, or rather inaction, you've caused the death of three people, soon to be four."

"I didn't kill them," Billy sobbed, still kneeling on the ground. "I didn't kill them; it was the sour gas in the air, in their water. That's what killed them."

"Potato, tomato. You can spin the story anyway you want, Billy, but they died on your watch. You might not have pulled the trigger, you didn't even buy the bullets or the gun, but you let them die when you could have stopped it."

"Well, if I would have filed any of those reports, nothing would have happened anyway. The government wouldn't have done anything 'cuz we're just a bunch of Indians that no one cares about. Even now, they know there's a much higher rate of cancer on our Rez, and some people have died, and what have they done? Nothing."

"You might be right, but that doesn't change the fact that *you* did nothing. Actually, you did more than nothing; you took bribes to look the other way, which is no different than a German soldier guarding Jews at the death camps during World War II. He probably didn't kill any of them himself, but he followed the orders that led to their deaths. What you did is no different."

"Yeah, but even if that soldier had stood up to the Nazis, he would have joined those Jews in the gas chamber."

"Probably, but at least he would have died knowing he had stood up against evil," the bird said, flying down to land on the ground beside where Billy knelt. "What have you done lately, except die knowing that you were a coward?"

Billy glared at the crow. "I wasn't a coward."

"Ha! You not only turned your back on what was happening, but you also took bribes. Unlike the German soldier, you didn't fear for your life for standing up for what was right; you only had to worry about whether you would lose your precious job and the side benefits."

Billy sobbed for a second more, knowing the bird was right. But then he realized something. He was dead. Somebody had killed him. Maybe that someone had something to do with DBA Resources. But was murder part of the business plan for the company? Billy didn't think so, but he wasn't sure.

Still, he couldn't figure anything out or get someone to help him figure it out if he just stayed on the ground and did nothing. Doing nothing seemed to be what had gotten him into this whole stupid mess in the first place. He had to move forward, and he knew only one way to do that.

Billy stood up and moved toward Aunt Kena's door. He tried the handle, but the door was locked. "Aunt Kena, let me in!" he shouted through the door. "Let me in so I can talk to you."

"Go away!" she shouted from behind the door.

"Come on, Aunt Kena, I need your help. I can't do this without you. No one else can see me but you."

"You should have thought of that before. You should have thought of that before you helped kill these poor kids."

Billy looked at the two Jennings kids through glass of the screen door. He smiled at them, and they both gave him a shy smile back. He knelt down in order to look them both in the eye. They took a single cautious step backward.

"I'm sorry," he said to the boy. And then he turned to the girl. "I'm sorry. It was my fault. I could have done something—well, it might not have helped you, I don't know. But I could have done something, and I didn't. I'm really sorry."

A few seconds passed as the little girl gazed at Billy intensely. And then she stepped forward and placed the palm of her hand on the screen. Billy brought his hand up, and he and the girl pressed their palms together through the screen.

The boy watched and then repeated the gesture with Billy's other hand.

As Billy placed both his hands against the screen, a great weight left him. He still felt sorrow because of their deaths, but the feeling was greatly tempered by a wondrous feeling of warmth and acceptance. The children had forgiven him for what he had done.

He nodded at the two kids, and they nodded back. Together, Kyle and his sister backed away from the door, and Billy stood up. "Thanks," he said. "I couldn't have gone on without you. And I know it's a lot to ask from you based on what I've done, but I need your help. I need you to let me in so I can talk to my aunt. If I talk to her, I might be able to set things right. I might not, but I have to try."

The kids looked at each other, and then the boy nodded at his sister. She reached out and opened the door for Billy. He stepped into the house, silently thanking the kids with a nod and a smile. He headed back to his auntie's bedroom.

He stormed into the room, surprising his aunt as she was helping Dale off the floor. She turned quickly, letting go of Dale and causing him to fall back down onto the floor.

"How did you get in here?" Aunt Kena demanded, her voice echoing like she was yelling into a canyon. Her height increased, and storm clouds formed on the ceiling above her head.

"The kids let me in," Billy said plainly.

His words seemed to soften his aunt, and she reverted to the old woman he recognized. She grabbed her chest and fell back on her butt on the bed. "They let you in?" she whispered. "That's not right. They're very angry with you, so why did they let you in?"

"Because I asked them to?"

"But you…"

"I know, Aunt Kena. I know what I did, and I told them I was sorry," Billy said, looking over his shoulder quickly and then back to his aunt. "They decided to—"

"—forgive you? They decided to forgive you." Aunt Kena sighed. She grabbed both of her braids and started to rub them. After a few seconds, she let them go and nodded her head. She stood up and looked deeply into Billy's eyes. "Still, they're only kids. And even though they've forgiven you, I won't. And I won't help you, Miss Pîyesî."

Billy nodded. "That's fine, Aunt Kena. I know you're busy and tired. So I'm not asking for your help." He pointed at Dale. "I'm asking for his help."

"Eyikos?" she said shocked. "What can he do?"

"He can drive. And he can interact with the real world, like a live human being."

"Ha. The boy can barely dress himself. Look what he's wearing."

"That's true, he's a bit of a mess, but he's the only one of us who seems to be alive and in a normal enough state to talk to people. Besides, right now I don't need him to talk to many people, I just need one thing from him."

"What's that?" Aunt Kena.

"I need him to find my body. I'm not going to get anywhere if no one knows that I've been murdered. Once that's discovered, maybe we can get some answers about this whole mess."

Aunt Kena frowned, her skepticism showing on her face. She took several deep breaths then tossed her braids over her shoulders. She reached down and yanked Dale up as if he was a little kid. She straightened him up and brushed off his shirt. She grabbed his hat from the floor and handed it to him. Dale took the hat, looked at her with fear and then looked at Billy. More fear came over his face.

Aunt Kena poked Dale in the chest and then pointed at Billy. "Eyikos, go help your cousin, Miss Pîyesî."

PART II

Fifteen

Dale was scared out of his mind. Sure, he was in his favorite place in the world, behind the wheel of his truck, but never had he driven his truck with a ghost by his side.

He knew a ghost was by his side because there was a flickering light in the passenger seat next to him, and every so often he heard a voice in his ear. The sound wasn't clear; it was full of static and it went in and out, like the time he and another cousin tried to use a pair of old walkie-talkies.

Aunt Kena told him the ghost was his cousin Billy and that he wasn't really a ghost but the essence of Billy's soul trapped between two worlds. Her explanation didn't set Dale's mind at ease. Her definition of Billy sounded like a ghost to him, and Dale knew that ghosts weren't a good thing. He had seen horror films and knew that ghosts, spirits or essences trapped between worlds could do a lot of damage. For example, maybe Billy could reach into his chest and stop his heart. Or maybe Billy could materialize into some kind of undead creature, like a zombie or vampire, and either suck his blood or eat his brains, turning him into a similar undead creature with a taste for blood and/or brains.

And how did he know this ghost was his cousin Billy in the first place? Ghosts were tricky creatures—that came with the territory of being trapped between worlds and willing to do anything to cross over to heaven or hell. So this ghost might not be Billy at all, but some kind of imposter that had fooled his Aunt Kena into forcing Dale to help him. Aunt Kena watched a lot of TV, much more than Dale, and she hadn't left her house since she broke her hip two years ago. So she was out of it most of the time, and Dale figured she was easy-pickings for any spiritual flim-flam man or spirit that showed up.

All of this was rumbling around in Dale's head when the ghost whispered in his ear, "Keep going another couple of miles, near a set of trees," which scared Dale out of his thoughts. He jerked in surprise, causing the truck to swerve to the right and left along the country road. Dale fought the truck, putting into action his defensive driving training, and steered the truck back on the straight and narrow.

His anxiety and fear finally got the best of him, and Dale yelled out in frustration. "Stop doing that, just stop!" he screamed, banging his fist against the dash. "This ain't easy to deal with, you know. A ghost in my truck, and my crazy aunt telling me I have to help you because our family demands it. Where the heck are we going anyway, could you tell me that?"

There was a pause in the static, and Dale couldn't tell if the ghost was talking to him and he couldn't hear it or if the ghost was just being quiet. After a few seconds, the voice returned, distant, like a shout in the woods, but clear nonetheless.

"Dale, I'm sorry to have mixed you up in this. I wouldn't do it if I had a choice in the matter," the voice said, sounding like Billy, but Dale still wasn't sure. He knew ghosts could be tricky, and he wasn't going to fall for any sob stories this spirit told him.

"Sure, you had a choice," Dale said. "You could have just died in peace and left the rest of us alone with our lives."

"That's the problem, I didn't die in peace. I died in violence, and I need to figure out why."

"Then go figure out why. You don't need my help. You're a damn ghost, and you should be able to get around without having to hitch a ride with me."

Again, another pause, this one longer, and Dale hoped the ghost had taken his advice and left. But it didn't; the voice floated up again

"I don't know how to do that kind of stuff," the voice said sheepishly.

This time it seemed that Billy was sitting right next to Dale, but Dale didn't hear what Billy said because he was surprised by the close proximity of the voice. Dale jumped in surprise, almost losing control of the truck again. Instead of driving on and risking a crash, he hit the brakes. He jammed the truck into park and reached across the passenger seat, punching his fist against the glove compartment. It flew open and Dale rummaged inside and quickly found what he was looking for, a small Bluetooth headset. He had worn it only for a few months because he finally realized that he looked like a tool with it on. Reluctantly, he clipped it on his right ear.

"Okay, ghost or spirit or whatever you are, if you're going to talk to me, you're going to have to speak to me through this Bluetooth because having your voice bounce back and forth isn't helping us reach our destination," Dale said angrily. "I want you to talk to me like any other caller, and don't speak to me until you figure it out. You got me?"

There was only silence, and Dale didn't know if the ghost had left or was trying to figure out a way to access the Bluetooth headset. But after about ten seconds, Dale heard a short chirp from the headset. He took that for a yes, that Billy had understood. Dale touched the earpiece and nodded, figuring that if the ghost was talking to him and he was talking back, at least wearing the Bluetooth might convince any witnesses that he wasn't losing his mind.

"I don't know if you're Billy or not, but my Aunt Kena says I gotta help you, and it's only because of her I'm helping you," Dale said. "So tell me where we're going, and let's get this stupid trip over with so I can get on with my life, okay?"

The earpiece chirped again, but no words came out. It chirped a few more times, then nothing. Dale shook his head. He knew he wasn't the brightest person in the world, but this ghost was hopeless. "Jeez. Come on. You're a ghost, you should be able to figure out some way to communicate with me."

A second later, a crow fluttered down and landed on the hood of Dale's truck. Dale shouted at it. "Get off my truck,

you stupid bird. Don't you dare take a crap on my paint job."
Dale beeped his horn several times.

The bird looked at him for a moment and then hopped
toward the windshield. Even though Dale was still worried
that the crow would ruin the paint, he was impressed with
the feat. The metal of the hood must have been pretty hot
because of the engine running, and the bird was hopping as if
it was just making its way across some soft grass.

The crow seemed to look directly into Dale's eyes,
staring at him until it reached the windshield. It tapped on
the glass a couple of times with its beak and then flew away,
staying on a level course, just a few feet above the road. The
bird flew ahead for about twenty feet and then flew back
toward the truck. It landed on the edge of the hood and
tapped it twice with its beak. Again, the bird flew away on the
exact course it had taken before, straight down the road at
a height that Dale could see it through his windshield.

The earpiece chirped in his ear twice before Dale
finally figured it out.

"Follow the bird!" he shouted. "You want me to follow
the bird?"

The earpiece chirped again.

Dale laughed, popped the truck into gear and started
to follow the bird. He drove slowly at first but then noticed
the bird was moving farther away, urging him to go faster. He
was doing about fifty miles per hour, and the bird was able to
stay in front of him.

Obviously, Dale thought, *this is no ordinary crow.*

Sixteen

Dale arrived at a wooded area a few miles down the road, and the crow slowed. It flew down and landed on a gate by the side of the road. The gate opened to a pair of old tire tracks that led into the trees. Dale recognized the area; it was a bush party hangout for the local teenagers. He knew there was a ravine behind the trees, a small creek, a makeshift fire pit and a lot of dark spaces to hide parked cars. For as long as anybody could remember, teenagers and slightly older youths would hang out here to drink, smoke and make out.

Even though he hadn't been the most popular kid in high school, Dale had been out here several times, drinking and smoking. He dreamt about making out but never got the chance.

The place was called Twin Bridges, but he had no idea where that name came from. There were no bridges or even remnants of bridges anywhere near the place.

Dale slowly turned his truck onto the access road, the long grass between the tire tracks scraping against the undercarriage of his truck. As he was driving along the path, the crow flew off the gate post and landed on the passenger mirror. On any other day, this would have been most unusual behavior for a bird, but this was not a usual day. Dale had already experienced the presence of his cousin Billy in the seat next to him. A ghost so useless that he had to get around by riding in a truck and using a crow to help with directions.

Dale carefully steered the truck toward the trees. Since it was the height of summer, the leaves of the trees were so thick that the shade made him turn on his headlights. He drove a few yards, when off to the side, he saw a flash, as if the sun was reflecting off a bright surface. He stopped the truck and leaned forward to look more closely through the windshield.

The object was hidden in some bushes, but Dale could see clearly what it was. A truck. There was a blare of static in his ear, and Dale saw the crow waving its wings. Dale turned the ignition off.

He reached for the door handle to leave the truck, but the static continued. The sound increased in volume, aggravating Dale the same way that rubbing of two pieces of Styrofoam together irritated him. He slapped his hand on the dash.

"If that noise is you guys talking to each other, then knock it off," he said to the crow and the flickering light in the passenger seat. "If you want my help, you're going to have to be quiet."

The static stopped, and the crow cocked its head at Dale. After waiting a few seconds, when he was sure they were going to be quiet and not talk among themselves, Dale nodded and stepped out of his truck.

The ground was soft, as if it had just rained, and he walked around the truck, heading to the one hidden behind the bushes. When he got to the vehicle, he saw that it looked similar to the band truck Billy drove. He couldn't confirm whether it was actually Billy's truck, but Dale figured it must be since the ghost in his seat claimed to be Billy.

Dale leaned against the passenger window, and placing both hands against the side of his head, looked inside the truck. He saw an empty coffee mug in the cup holder, a pair of sunglasses on the dash and a bunch of papers strewn on the passenger seat, but that was all. He didn't see anything to confirm that it was Billy's truck.

Dale reached down to try the door handle but then stopped and pulled his hand away. If the ghost was Billy, and if it was true that he had died violently, Dale realized he shouldn't touch the truck in case he left some of his fingerprints behind. He didn't want to be considered a suspect.

He stepped away from the truck, looking around him to check if anybody else was in the area. No one. Except for the crow still perched on the side mirror of his truck. The bird squawked once and then flew down a path. It landed on a branch hanging low to the ground and squawked again.

Dale knew he was being told to follow the bird. So he did, gingerly picking his way down the path as the crow alternately hopped and flew in front of him. The path led down the ravine, toward the creek and the fire-pit area

The wind blew gently through the trees, and the creek burbled in the distance. The sun was high and peeked through the leaves every so often, but Dale felt a chill in the air. The kind of cold that seeps deep into your bones, a cold rarely felt in the prairies.

When Dale reached the fire pit, he saw a small mound near the creek. It looked like a bundle of discarded clothes. But as he got closer, he knew that the clothes had not been discarded; someone was still wearing them. The sound of the wind and the creek permeated the air, but Dale heard another sound in the background. Buzzing.

The crow flew a few feet and landed on a large rock next to the clothes. The bird screeched once. At that moment, Dale knew exactly what he was looking at. He knew he should just walk away and leave the body where it was, forget everything that happened to him today and drive back to his basement apartment in the city where it was safe and no one knew him.

But, as he had done when he thought he had run over someone, Dale knew he couldn't leave. He wasn't brave, and he wasn't as stupid as some people thought him to be, but he wasn't a coward, either.

If the body on the ground was Billy's, Dale had to find out. He didn't know what would happen and what he would do after he got that confirmation, but he still had to look at the body to make sure.

He walked up to the body until he was only about five feet away. From that distance, he could see that it was Billy. He was dead. And he had a small hole in the center of his forehead. There was a lot of dried blood around the hole, and flies were buzzing around the hole, some flying in and out of the opening.

Dale dropped to his knees and emptied his stomach. Static blared in his ears, but he barely heard it.

Seventeen

Billy watched from a distance as Dale sat in the backseat of the RCMP cruiser with his feet hanging out the open door. Dale was drinking from a bottle of water while a female Mountie stood next to him, her elbow leaning against the car roof. She looked familiar to Billy, but he couldn't remember her name.

She talked gently to Dale, and the tone of her voice made it obvious she knew him.

Billy had been surprisingly impressed by Dale's actions. After he had thrown up and dealt with the grief of finding his cousin's body, Dale had regained his composure and took a deep breath.

He looked about the air. "I'm real sorry you're dead, Billy," he said softly. "We didn't see much of each other in the past few years, but you always treated me okay. You were a good guy."

And then Dale walked slowly back to his truck. Billy started to say something to his cousin, but Dale waved him away. It was obvious he wanted to be alone for a moment, even though he knew a ghost or spirit of some kind was nearby. When Dale reached his truck, he got out his cellphone and called the authorities.

It took them about twenty minutes to get to the creek. And in that entire time, Dale just sat inside his truck, the windows rolled down, staring out through the windshield. When he heard the sirens in the distance, he sighed, climbed out of the truck and directed the vehicles in.

The first to arrive was the RCMP cruiser, and instead of pulling onto the access road, it did a U-turn and parked on the side of the road so that the ambulance and fire truck could get into the area. The female Mountie got out of the cruiser, greeted Dale and then gestured for him to show her and the other emergency workers where the body was located.

Dale led them to the truck and then took them down the ravine, where Billy's body lay. When the officials caught sight of the body, the paramedics were the first ones to move. They ran toward it, squatted down on their knees and checked for vital signs. Billy felt a little uneasy seeing strangers messing with his body, but he was no longer in it and couldn't use it anymore. So there was nothing he could do to intervene.

When the paramedics confirmed the man was dead, they stepped back. The Mountie took over. She ordered everybody away, making them stand back at least twenty feet away from the body. And then she walked around the body, carefully watching where she placed her feet and making sure not to disturb anything around the body. While she did this, she took copious notes, flipping page after page in her small notebook.

When she completed her writing, she asked everyone to leave the ravine then made a call on her cellphone. Billy could see that she paid close attention to Dale, walking behind him to the main road. When they reached the main road, the emergency workers all returned to their vehicles. The firefighters left immediately, but the paramedics stayed behind.

The Mountie guided Dale to her cruiser, opened the back door and asked him to sit, but she left the door open. She offered him a bottle of water and started asking questions. The paramedics watched from a distance, seemingly there to provide protection for the Mountie. But Billy didn't think she would need it.

"So Dale," the Mountie said. "You found the body when?"

"Like I said, about forty-five minutes ago," he said with a sigh.

"And the first thing you did was call us?" she asked. "You did nothing else? Didn't touch the body or anything?"

"Touch the body? Are you crazy? Why would I touch the body?"

"To find out if he was dead or not? To grab him and cry in grief? To check his pockets in case he had the money that you owed him?"

"What! I never checked his pockets. Why would I do that? He didn't owe me any money!"

The cop shrugged but also noted Dale's reaction in her notebook. Billy wasn't sure if Dale noticed her movements, but he sure did.

"That was only an example," the cop said, obviously lying. "You'd be surprised, and shocked, at the number of reasons people come up with to touch a dead body."

"Well, I didn't touch the body."

"Why not?" the cop asked. "Why didn't you grab him in grief? You said that he was your cousin Billy. Why didn't you try to see if he was alive or see if you could resuscitate him?"

"Because I was afraid to," Dale said after a pause. "I've never seen a dead body before."

"Never?" the cop asked, her pen busy on her notebook.

"Never."

"So that's why you threw up?"

Dale's head snapped up in surprise. He looked at the Mountie for a few seconds and then his shoulders slumped and he looked away. "Yeah, I threw up," he said, shamefully.

"No other reason for throwing up? No guilt or remorse?"

This time Dale turned more slowly to look at her, his face showing the horror of what she must have thought about him. "I didn't kill Billy. Why would I kill Billy?'

"I don't know," the cop said and shrugged. "People can always find a reason to kill someone. Doesn't even have to be much. Especially with family members."

"I didn't kill Billy," Dale said, the anger rising in his voice. He started to get up. The two paramedics noticed Dale's movements and began to move in his direction. But the cop saw them out of the corner of her eye, and without looking at them, waved them away with the hand that held the notebook.

She took a half step toward Dale, and with her other hand, she pressed on his shoulder and gently pushed him back. He didn't fight her, just sat down on the backseat of the cruiser.

"Take it easy," she said to Dale, lifting her hand off him as he sat down again. "No need to get upset." She stepped back and wrote quickly in her notebook

"No need to get upset?" Dale said, tears forming in his eyes. "I just found my cousin dead, and you tell me there's no reason to get upset?"

"That's understandable, but there's no reason to get upset at me; I'm just doing my job."

"Yeah, which is to think I killed Billy when I didn't."

"Why do you think I think you killed Billy?"

"Because you keep asking me these questions about searching his body for money or if I threw up because I felt guilty or remorseful for killing Billy."

The Mountie took more notes. "Do you feel guilty and remorseful for killing Billy?" she asked in a soft voice.

"No!" Dale said.

"So you don't feel guilty and remorseful for killing Billy?"

"No—I mean, yes—I mean, no, I don't feel guilty and remorseful because I *didn't* kill Billy."

"You sure about that?"

"Yes. I'm sure about that."

"Sure about what? Not being guilty or remorseful, or killing Billy?"

"I didn't kill Billy!" Dale shouted. He stood up quickly. This time the two paramedics headed toward the cruiser. But the cop had everything under control.

She placed a hand on Dale's shoulder and squeezed tightly.

"Take it easy, Dale. Because if you don't, I'm going to have to cuff you and lock you in the backseat. And I won't turn on the air conditioner. It's pretty hot out today."

Dale looked at the cop, surprised at her threat. But he sat down.

The paramedics arrived at the cruiser. "Everything okay, Sara?" asked the larger of the two men.

Sara. That was her name, Dale thought. But then he saw her nametag that read *Constable S. Sara*. He didn't think her name could be "Sara Sara," but then again, he never thought he'd be questioned by the police because he found the body of his cousin.

"Everything's fine, Mike," Constable Sara said with annoyance. "I've got things under control."

"You sure?" asked Mike, giving Dale a stern look.

119

"I'm fine," she said without turning to look at Mike, which Billy could see annoyed the paramedic. "I've got it under control."

"Come on, Mike," the other paramedic said, grabbing Mike by the shoulder and pulling him back. "Let her do her job."

Mike stood still for a moment, fighting his partner, but only for a second. Then he reluctantly backed away, still looking hard at Dale.

When they left, Sara leaned in again to ask Dale another question.

Dale looked at her with a smug smile on his face. "Yeah, why don't you have me cuffed in the backseat already? If you think I killed Billy, then you should have cuffed me. But you didn't, so that tells me you don't think I killed Billy. Ha."

The cop smiled at Dale. It was a bright smile, the kind of smile a girl gives a guy at the bar that tells him she likes him. "That could be right. But I could also believe you killed Billy, but I didn't cuff you and stick you in the back of the car because I wanted to calm you down and make you believe that I don't think you killed Billy so you'll give something away that will prove to me that you actually did kill Billy."

Dale's face turned red, looking like a teenager being caught masturbating. "I don't want to talk to you anymore."

The cop was still smiling. "Sorry, you have no choice in the matter. So tell me again, when did you find…"

She didn't get a chance to finish her question because she noticed that the two paramedics were on the move again.

But they weren't interested in her or Dale. They were looking at the road, watching a line of vehicles pull up.

There were three more cruisers, an unmarked cop car as well as a non-descript gray van.

The cruisers parked alongside the road while the van pulled onto the access road and followed the trail into the woods. Six uniformed cops got out of the cruisers; three followed the van, while the other three spread out to isolate the crime scene. Three plainclothes cops got out of the unmarked car, and only one man followed the van. The other two cops, an older man with salt-and-pepper hair and a porn-star mustache, and a younger fellow, headed toward Sara. Sara met them about halfway, away from Dale, a few feet in front of her cruiser.

The older cop didn't introduce himself so Billy realized they probably knew each other. He hovered around the group of cops to eavesdrop on their conversation.

"This the guy who found the body?" the older cop asked, gesturing with a nod toward Dale.

"Yeah, name is Dale Ghostkeeper," Sara said. "The victim is apparently his cousin Billy Ghostkeeper."

"He involved in the death?"

Sara paused. She looked at Dale for several seconds and then turned back to the two cops. "No," she said, shaking her head.

"You sure?"

"Pretty much," she said. "I've seen Dale around the Rez a few times. He's harmless."

"Harmless folks have a way of becoming harmful pretty fast."

Billy could tell from the tone of the older cop's voice that he wasn't judging Sara's comments; it was just a statement of fact.

"Yeah, but Dale really is harmless. He's pretty upset that his cousin was killed. Puked and everything. Also got righteously angry when I suggested that he killed his cousin."

"What about the gangbanger outfit?" the younger plainclothes cop asked. "Looks like he could be trouble based on what he's wearing. He one of them?"

Billy knew the cop was asking if Dale was a member of the local gang.

Sara shook her head. "Dale? No way. This is just a look for him. He doesn't even live on the Rez. Lives in the city; does some sort of computer work from what I gather."

"What's he doing on the Rez then?" the older cop asked.

"Visiting his aunt," Sara said. "He comes by once a week to make sure she's okay. Brings her groceries and other stuff."

"What about the aunt?" the younger cop asked.

Sara smiled, holding back laughter. "Kena. She's harmless. An elder and some kind of shaman they say, but she can barely get around. Heard she broke her hip a few years ago and hasn't left her house since. I drop by once in a while to check up on her."

The other cop seemed surprised at her statement. "Why the heck would you do that?"

"Part of my job, I guess. Got to keep an eye on these old folks around here. Don't want them getting some kind of attack and then dying in their homes all alone. Most of them don't have nephews like Dale to check up on them.

The older cop nodded. "Okay, good work, Constable," he said. Billy wasn't sure whether he was talking about how she handled the crime scene or that she regularly checked on some of the elders on the Rez. "So do we keep cousin Dale, or do we let him go?"

"Let him go," she said without pausing. "He only found the body; he's not a suspect."

"Okay, ask him some more questions to see if his story sticks. And if it does, let him go," the older cop said, turning to look at the patch of trees behind him. "So tell me about the body."

"Male, Native, mid to late thirties. Lying face up at the bottom of the ravine, near the creek bed. Looks like a bullet hole in the middle of his forehead."

"Short or long-range shot?"

"Seems to be short range."

"Any weapons or casings nearby?"

"Nothing. But I only did a preliminary check near the body. I didn't want to contaminate the scene before you guys got here."

"Good. Tell me more."

Sara thought for a second and then flipped her notebook to another page. "Spotted some flesh and brain matter on the ground near where the body was found. There's also a lot of blood underneath the head so I'm thinking the exit wound is pretty big."

"You find the bullet anywhere, stuck in a tree or something?"

Sara shook her head. "Nope. But I didn't look around for too long. Like I said, I didn't want to contaminate the scene."

The older cop nodded. "Any ideas on the type of weapon used?"

Billy thought the older cop was not only trying to get more information, but he was also testing Sara.

"Don't like to speculate," she said.

The older cop's reaction—the slight smile on his face and the little nods—made Billy realize she was passing the test with flying colors.

"Don't worry about speculating, Constable. Give it your best shot, so to speak."

"Probably a semi-automatic pistol of some kind. Powerful one, but I won't guess on the make or caliber."

"So who in this area would have that kind of weapon?" the older cop asked.

"We would," blurted out the other plainclothes cop, not realizing that he wasn't being asked the question.

The older cop sighed and rolled his eyes. "Besides *us*," he said with a disappointed tone. "Constable?"

"Gangs," she said without hesitation. "They have guns like that."

"Bingo," the older cop said, snapping his fingers.

Billy had the same thought, realizing he had his first lead in discovering who had murdered him.

Eighteen

Dale was driving his truck again, this time much more slowly, like a senior citizen heading home from church. He was glad to be away from the bush party area, now a crime scene.

Constable Sara had interviewed him again, asking the same questions over and over, but using different words. He answered each of them the same way he had the first time, also using most of the same words. Sara wrote down his answers in a notebook, cracking open another when she filled all the pages of the first one.

Finally, she told Dale he could go.

But Dale couldn't leave because the forensic guys were going over his truck the same way the female constable had gone over his story. Meticulously. They had to make sure no incriminating evidence remained in the vehicle.

When the all-clear was finally given, several hours had passed. The sun was now low in the western sky, the tall poplars on the prairie grasslands casting long shadows.

More vehicles had arrived near the bush area during that time, most of them lookeeloos who had heard via the grapevine that something exciting was going on at Twin Bridges.

There was not much to see, just a bunch of parked vehicles with flashing lights—most of the action was taking place down in the ravine by the creek. But since there was really nothing much to do on the Rez, it was excitement enough.

Dale drove without any music blaring, trying to figure out how he could get rid of the smell of fingerprint dust from the truck's upholstery. The fine gray stuff was everywhere; he'd have to spend a few hundred bucks on a complete detailing package in order to get his truck back to its mint condition.

He was also beat, exhausted not just by the events at Aunt Kena's house or finding Billy's body in the ravine, but also because of the constable's relentless questioning. After the plainclothes cops left to check out the body and Sara returned to questioning him, Dale finally recognized her.

He had seen her at the band community store a few months earlier. He had just been at Aunt Kena's house and was buying a few things before he returned to the city. Sara was in line ahead of him, in her civvies, and was buying potato chips, a can of Coke and a movie.

Dale wasn't the kind of man to talk to women out of the blue, but he couldn't help but notice the movie she was buying. "That's a great movie," he said.

She turned and smiled. It set his heart pounding. "I know. I saw it years ago, but when I saw it on the shelf here, I had to buy it."

"Yeah, I really thought that Callum Keith Rennie was a real guitar player because of that movie; I didn't know he was only acting."

"Yeah, it was pretty cool," she said, turning to get her change from the clerk.

Dale knew that in a few seconds she would be out of his life forever and he couldn't believe the words that came out of his mouth next. "You don't want any company to watch it with, do ya?"

She turned and smiled at him again, glancing at his purchases. "Thanks, but I'll be okay. I think you already have your hands full."

She then left the store, and at that moment Dale didn't feel bad for being rejected. At least he gave it a shot for once. But when he saw the smile on the clerk's face, he knew why she had made that comment. Dale had forgotten that among the many items he had purchased was a *Playboy* magazine. He immediately dropped his stuff on the counter and left the store, hearing the clerk break out in huge guffaws behind him.

Dale banged his fist against the dashboard, remembering the incident and realizing that she was also the cop who had just interviewed him. "Dammit all to hell!" he shouted.

The Bluetooth earpiece that he had forgotten he was wearing chirped in his ear.

"I'm sorry about all that," Billy said, his voice coming across crisp and clear.

"You shut up. I don't wanna hear from you again!" Dale shouted. "All I want to do is to go home, get some sleep and forget this day ever happened."

"I could say the same thing, but I can't. I'm dead."

"No shit, Sherlock. I know you're dead. I found your stupid body in the fricking ravine, and now the cops think I killed you."

"They don't think you killed me. That lady cop said you were harmless, that you couldn't hurt anyone."

"That's supposed to make me feel better, everybody thinking that I'm harmless?"

"Of course it should."

"But I'm a hard-ass dude, man," Dale said, not really believing it.

"No, you're not, Dale. You're a bit of a poser."

"Great, that's nice of you to say. And this from a guy who says he needs my help."

"Well, I do need your help."

"No, you don't. You're doing fine without me."

"No, I'm not. I was murdered," Billy said. "I was shot in the head and left for dead in a stupid ravine by Twin Bridges."

Dale tried not to laugh at his dead cousin's last comment, but he couldn't help it.

"What's so funny?" Billy asked.

"Nothing," Dale said. He slowed down even more when he realized that he was about to pull near the edge of the village, across the Rez line where a bunch of stores—a liquor store, drugstore and bar—sold stuff you couldn't buy on the Rez.

"No, really, tell me what's funny."

"It's just that when you said 'I was shot in the head and left for dead,'" Dale sang in a tough hip-hop voice, "it sounded like some kind of gangsta rap song."

Billy gave a short laugh, but then realized where they were. "Pull over, Dale, I need your help."

"No way, man. I'm going home."

"You can't go home, I need to finish this."

"Then finish it. But leave me out of it. I'm not a part of this."

"Of course you are. You're family."

"Ha. Family. When's the last time you even called me? When's the last time you helped out Aunt Kena? I go over to her house every week and have to deal with her crazy shaman crap, but you don't even show up until you're dead. And I live in the city. You used to live on the Rez less than five minutes away from her place, but not once did you look in on her."

Billy sighed. "I know, I know, and I was wrong. But I need your help. I can't do this without you."

"Sure, you can. Before you couldn't even talk to me in my earpiece, and now you're as clear as a bell. How the heck did that happen?"

There was no response. And Dale knew that Billy was thinking about it. "I honestly don't know how that happened," Billy finally said.

"Well, you must have done something because before you couldn't do it, and now you can speak to me clearly. You don't know the extent of your powers, so chances are you don't need me. You can handle things on your own." Dale turned the truck into the bar parking lot and then reached over and opened the door.

"See you later, Billy. I'd like to say it was good to see you today, but that would be lying. Sorry you're dead, but it's not my fault."

"You gotta help me, Dale," Billy pleaded. "I can't do this without your help."

"Then you just got to believe in yourself. Which I'll admit is kind of hard, seeing you're a ghost and all, and most people don't believe in ghosts."

"Please, Dale, help me."

"Give me one good reason why I should, and I will."

There was a pause, and then Billy reminded him of what happened with Gar all those years ago. Dale remembered only parts of the incident, when Gar first hit him, and then everything went blank. He did remember, though, the pain afterward and how everyone told him Billy had saved his life. Billy never really acted like he had saved his life; he always seemed to be angry when anyone talked about the incident, and he blamed Dale for getting himself beat up.

"That's a low blow," Dale said. "Besides, you could have stopped Gar from hitting me in the first place."

"I could have, but I didn't. At least I didn't let him kill you. That's got to count for something."

Dale sat quiet for a moment and then shook his head. He was still in shock at discovering Billy's body in the ravine. And he was humiliated and exhausted by the cop's questioning. But he couldn't deny what Billy had done for him those many years ago. He was truly sad that Billy was dead. So in the same way that he had decided to help Aunt Kena, he would now help Billy.

"Okay, but only this one time. Once we deal with this, I don't want you haunting me for the rest of my life, as if we were characters in some kind of bad TV show, you got me? We do this, and then I go home and live my life in peace."

"Okay. Thanks, Dale. I won't forget this."

"No, I want you to forget this when we're done and leave me alone," Dale said. "Now, what am I supposed to do?"

"Well, the cops were talking about the gun that shot me, and they said only two types of folks in this area have that kind of gun: cops and gangs."

Dale took a deep breath. "Geez, I hope you aren't asking me what I think you are asking."

"Yep. I need you to go into the bar and talk to Gar."

"What about your stupid bird? It seems pretty smart. Can't that crow talk to Gar for you? Gar will be drunk, and it won't bother him if a bird talks to him."

"The crow doesn't even like talking to me, so sorry, Dale, it's gotta be you. You have to talk to Gar and figure out if any of his guys are involved."

Dale shook his head, wishing he was back in the community store buying as much pornography as he could carry while Constable Sara, the clerk and the rest of the Rez stood there and laughed at him. At least that was safe. But he gave his word to Billy.

"I'll do it, Billy, but I think it's a stupid idea because if Gar and his boys were involved in your murder, chances are I'll be joining you in that ravine before the sun comes up tomorrow."

Nineteen

As soon as Dale entered the bar, Billy knew he had made a mistake in asking his cousin to talk to Gar. The place was busy, not packed, but enough people were around to make it difficult for Dale if he had to leave quickly. About a third of the people in the bar were gang members. Gathered around an old pool table at the back, the gang members were holding court like a group of unruly knights. They were drinking beer and laughing loudly, grabbing at the waitress when she walked by, and anyone not related to the gang moved out their way, so as not to spark them into anger.

Rowdy and drunk they were, but in a few seconds, they could turn into an angry mob of well-trained fighters. They liked to style themselves as great Aboriginal warriors, but they were actually just thugs.

Billy thought of telling Dale to get out of the bar, but it was too late.

Dale hadn't attracted attention when he first entered the bar, only a few looks here and there. But as soon as he walked to the back of the bar, near the pool table, nobody could miss him.

Everyone on the Rez knew who Dale was, and even though they probably made fun of him behind his back, some of them respected him for what he did for his aunt. Despite the infiltration of gangs and the Rez gradually losing its Cree culture, the elders in the community were still respected.

Even so, if anybody entered the inner sanctum of the gang area, even accidently, they were pushed around and spit at, and then, if they were lucky, tossed out into the main area of the bar. But Dale, who was part of the gang's lore because of the incident in high school, caused so much surprise with his appearance that the gang members stepped out of his way and allowed him to enter their circle.

The bar went silent, and some of the patrons wisely downed their drinks and left before things got too dangerous. The bartender grabbed the wireless phone and held onto it, ready to dial 911 in case things got out of hand.

Gar was lining up a shot, his back to Dale, so he hadn't noticed Dale come in. The other eight or so gang members involved in the game stepped back when Dale came up behind Gar.

As Gar was pulling back his pool cue to take his shot, he glanced behind him and saw Dale. He jerked his pool cue in surprise just as it connected with the ball, and he missed his shot. The cue ball flew widely around the table, hitting other balls that weren't part of Gar's game plan and then fell into one of the pockets, scratching.

"Holy shit, it's Dale Ghostkeeper," Gar said, standing up quickly and smiling at Dale. "How you been, buddy, it's been awhile." He may have sounded pleased and happy to see Dale, but everyone knew he was only putting up a front. Everyone, even Dale, was aware that Gar was playing with Dale, setting up the scene so that the violence to come would be more dramatic.

And this situation would end in violence. Billy knew that. He was aware that even Dale knew the outcome, but Gar was their only lead in Billy's death and they had to follow it, no matter what.

Gar looked around, pointing his pool cue at the various gang members around him. "Somebody get Dale a beer," he said, pretending to be a friendly host. "You wanna beer don't you, Dale?"

Dale, obviously shaken and afraid, slowly shook his head. "No, I really don't want a beer."

"What? You can't refuse a beer," Gar said, his voice friendly but with an icy tone creeping in. "You walk into my place uninvited, which is okay for the most part because you and I go way back. But then you refuse my hospitality of a beer; now that ain't nice. Tradition says that if you refuse a brother's hospitality when you enter his place, that shows you're an enemy and not a friend. You do want me to think of you as a friend, don't ya?"

Although Gar phrased it as a question, it wasn't really one. A few more customers left the bar, and the bartender dialed the 9 in 911. Some members of the gang looked at each other and smiled; things were starting to get interesting.

"Take the beer," Billy said in Dale's earpiece. "You want him on your side for the moment."

Dale twitched at the sound of Billy's voice. Everyone, including Gar, saw the twitch and thought it was because of fear. And it was, partly. Their smiles grew even larger as they smelled the fear.

"Sure, Gar, I'll have a beer," Dale said quickly. "I just thought you were going to make one of your boys give me one of theirs, and I didn't want to deprive them of their refreshment."

Gar laughed, deep yet mean. "Deprive them of their refreshment? Ha! You kill me, Dale. You always have. But there's plenty of fresh beers lying around so you can have one, and no one will be deprived of refreshment because of it."

Gar pointed his pool cue at a line of full beer bottles on a table. Dale grabbed one. He looked at the beer and then held it out. Gar thought he was holding it out for a toast so he tapped the tip of his bottle against Dale's.

"*Salute,*" he said, taking a sip.

Dale looked at Gar, and Billy could see his hand shaking as he held the bottle. Everyone could. But after a second, Dale took a drink.

Gar watched and then nodded. "So, Dale, don't get me wrong, I've got nothing against old friends coming over to say hi and enjoying a beer with me, but I'm curious about your visit."

"I…uh…I, wanted to talk to you. I mean, I was hoping we could have a chat," he stammered.

"About what?"

Dale paused, cleared his throat and swallowed. "It's about Billy. I want to ask you about Billy."

The silence in the room was so intense that it almost hurt, like a sudden drop in air pressure. Based on the shocked looks on the faces of the other gang members, it was obvious that Dale had crossed a major line by mentioning Billy's name.

Gar's eyes narrowed, and any jocularity he had pasted on his face vanished. His right eye twitched slightly, like a crazy gunslinger about to go for his six-shooter.

"As much as I like to talk about…your cousin," Gar hissed through his teeth, "you can see that I'm busy right now. I'm in the middle of a game here, so I'm going to let my boys handle this for me."

Billy knew Dale had been dismissed and now faced a beating. Not a serious one, but enough to keep him out of action for several weeks. Bones would be broken, but no permanent damage done.

A few of the younger gang members moved toward Dale, and Gar leaned down to shoot pool again, already forgetting about Dale.

And then Billy had an idea. He wasn't sure his plan would work, but it might give them some extra time.

Dale might still get beat up in the end, but they might also get a few answers out of Gar. Billy knew that Gar loved to play pool, fancied himself some kind of shark. And he had the right. Gar was good, the best on the Rez. Billy had even heard that Gar had won some tournaments in the city. But Billy had to try anyway.

"Challenge him to a game of pool," Billy shouted in Dale's earpiece.

Dale jumped at the sound, and the gang thought he was trying to escape. A couple of them grabbed him by the arms, holding him tight. "Sorry, you're going nowhere," one of them said with a laugh.

"What?" Dale asked. "What did you say?"

"I said you're not going nowhere, you stupid idiot."

"Challenge him to a game of pool," Billy said again.

"But I don't play pool," Dale said.

"Of course you don't play pool," the gang member said. "But we'll play with you for a while."

"No. Challenge Gar to a game," Billy repeated. "Bet him something, and maybe we'll get some answers. I'll help you win."

"But you can't help me," Dale said.

"No one's going to help you now," said the gang member.

Gar stood up and banged his fist on the table. "Why is that piece of crap still here? I thought I told you guys to take care of him, but you guys keep yammering, ruining my game."

"I challenge you to a game," Dale said haltingly, still pinned between two gang members.

Gar blinked but didn't move. He stared at Dale for a moment. He then stepped forward and stood a few inches from Dale. He tapped Dale on the chest with the tip of his pool cue, leaving blue cue dust on Dale's shirt.

"You wanna challenge *me* to a game of pool?" Gar asked.

Dale nodded. "Yeah, I hear you're pretty good. I wanna see how good."

"I don't play just *anyone*, ya know. You have to make it worth my while."

Dale thought for a few seconds. "What should I bet?" he asked Billy, but everyone thought he was asking Gar.

"Don't ask me," Gar said with a laugh. "Figure it out for yourself."

"Bet him to answer some questions about me. Questions about my murder," Billy said.

"I can't do that, that's stupid," Dale said.

"Darn right it's stupid," Gar said, thinking Dale was addressing him. "Coming in here was one of the stupidest ideas ever, and you're making it even worse."

"Figure something out fast, or you're a dead man," Billy said.

Gar was about to dismiss Dale again, leaving him to an even more serious beating.

But Dale spoke up.

"Anything. I'll bet anything."

"Anything?" Gar said, a hint of confusion in his voice. "What the hell does that mean?"

"It means no-holds-barred. Whoever wins the game can ask the loser to do anything. Or the winner gets to do anything to the loser or ask him anything, no questions asked."

Gar leaned back against the table, tapping the pool cue against his chest. "Anything?"

"Anything," Dale said with determination.

"You know, that's actually pretty interesting, Dale. Probably the most interesting bet anyone has ever made with me." He stood up straight and gestured to his gang members to let Dale go. Gar then spit into his right hand and held it out to Dale.

"Anything," Gar said.

"Anything," Dale replied. He spit in his hand and grabbed Gar's.

Gar squeezed hard, trying to break Dale's hand. "Best two of out three."

"Deal," Dale said, the pain obvious in his voice.

Gar squeezed for another second and then tossed Dale's hand away. "Alrighty then. Rack 'em up."

Twenty

One of Gar's gangbangers racked up the pool balls into the typical eight-ball triangle. Gar grabbed a pool cue from the rack hanging on the wall and handed it to Dale.

"Ladies first," he said with a smile, and then he stepped back, leaning against the wall. The rest of the gangbangers watched with glee, most of them knowing that Dale stood no chance against Gar.

Dale took a deep breath and leaned over the table to take his first shot. This is stupid, he thought. He hadn't played pool in years, and even then he was a terrible player. He really hoped Billy had some clue about what he was doing.

Dale wasn't optimistic though. From his point of view, Billy was a terrible ghost. He had none of the abilities that the ghosts, or the undead or spirits, had in the movies Dale had seen. Billy couldn't levitate or moan, and he could appear to only one person. He didn't suck blood or eat brains, nor could he change shape or control the cosmos in any way.

He couldn't do anything cool. Heck, he even had trouble communicating with Dale, and he couldn't transport himself from place to place; he had to get rides everywhere. So lame!

Billy couldn't scare anyone, not even Dale anymore. But Dale hoped his cousin got his ghostly stuff together fast because if he didn't…well, Dale didn't want to think of how Gar would define *anything*. The guy was pretty twisted.

So Dale took a deep breath and made his shot. The cue ball rolled quickly, easily breaking the rack. The balls all bounced around the table, and one of them fell into a corner pocket.

"Nice break," Gar said with an appreciative nod. He walked over to the pocket and pulled out the ball. He held it up. "Number six. That makes you solids. Make your next shot." He dropped the ball back into the pocket.

Dale was impressed with his break, though not entirely sure if Billy had anything to do with it. He looked about the table and then saw the four sitting near the side pocket. He walked over to the cue ball on the other side of the table and lined up to shoot at the four.

Just as Dale pulled back his cue to shoot, Gar spoke. "Really hope you're not hustling me, Dale. That wouldn't be nice."

His words distracted Dale, and the cue ball bounced off the four but sent his ball away from the pocket. He winced. "Nice job," he said quietly to Billy.

"Relax," Billy said. "I'm working on it. Moving objects isn't easy."

"Great, that's helpful," Dale said.

"It's very helpful," Gar said, thinking Dale was talking to him. "In fact, it's probably the best move you've done for me so far."

Gar sank the next ball, a ten. And then for the next five minutes, he ran the table, sinking every one of his balls. On his last shot, sinking the eight ball in a far corner pocket, he didn't even look at his shot. He just stared at Dale, his eyes smiling.

"That's one to nothing. Halfway to *anything*," he said, after sinking the eight ball. "Rack 'em up again."

As one of the gangbangers gathered the balls and began to rack them, Gar walked over and stood next to Dale. He rocked back and forth on his heels and toes. "You know, I haven't had this much fun in a long time. So I really appreciate you showing up like this, Dale. You've made my day. But the best part has nothing to do with pool."

Gar leaned closer to Dale. "Ask me what the best part is."

Dale sighed, mentally cursing Billy and his Aunt Kena for getting him into this mess. "What's the best part, Gar?" he said mechanically.

"The best part is figuring out what I'm going to make you do or do to you," he said, tapping Dale on the shoulder. "You have no idea what's going through my mind. I mean, it's such a different bet; it's so twisted that thinking about it so much might affect my game."

The balls were racked, and the gangbanger tapped the triangle on the felt to let the players know. Gar stepped up and lined up his break shot. As he pulled back his cue, he turned to Dale. "But the bet isn't going to affect my game at all. In fact, it's making me play better."

The cue ball hit the rack with a massive crack. The balls exploded all around the table, three of them falling into various pockets. Dale groaned as Gar fist-pumped the air, calling out stripes again.

Gar sank all the stripes again without fail. And he was lining up to shoot the eight ball on a bank into the side pocket. For Dale, it would be an impressive shot. But for Gar, it was average.

"Come on, Billy," Dale whispered to the air. "You gotta help me. Come on, Billy."

Gar looked up at Dale as he readied his shot. "Billy can't help you now, Dale. After this shot, your life is mine, and it isn't going to be a pretty one."

Gar's smile sent shivers down Dale's spine. Dale clenched his teeth, and in his mind he shouted out Billy's name in anger. A second later, the room seemed to grow cold. Dale's ears popped as the air pressure changed.

Gar took his shot, the cue ball hitting the eight cleanly. The eight bounced off the rail and headed straight for the side pocket. But when the ball was within a couple of inches from the pocket, the ball just stopped. Dead. As if something had blocked it.

Gar jumped up in disbelief. "What the heck? That should have gone in!" he shouted, looking around. "Something's wrong with this table. Did one of you put a beer on it? One of you must have and wrecked my shot." He ranted and raved some more.

"Yesssss," Dale hissed to himself. "Hope that was you, Billy."

"It was," Billy said in his ear. "I don't know how, but I did it."

"Keep it up, then."

"I'll try."

Dale went over to line up a shot on the two ball. Gar saw him and dashed over, grabbing his cue. "What the heck do you think you're doing?" he snapped.

"Taking my shot," Dale said without flinching. "You missed."

"I didn't miss. The table is messed up and screwed with my shot."

Dale shrugged. "Not my fault. It's your table, not mine."

"Yeah, but I'm taking my shot again."

Dale backed away from Gar and adjusted his ball cap. "Seriously, dude? You're kicking my ass. You're down to your last ball, and you missed but you want to try it again? Just wait until I miss this one, and you'll get another chance."

For a moment Gar was confused. He looked back and forth between his gang members, but none of them would look him in the eye. He grunted and then sucked back his

GHOST DETECTIVE

anger. "Okay, you piece of shit," he snarled. "Go make your shot and miss. Just remember that you'll pay extra for that attitude of yours."

Dale felt his sphincter tighten in fear, but on the outside he only shrugged. And then he lined up his shot. Before he made his move, he looked up to the ceiling and said a quiet prayer to Billy.

He shut his eyes and made his shot. Much to his and everyone else's surprise, the ball went in the pocket. It wasn't pretty, but the two ball went in.

And so did the rest of the balls. Dale ran the table all the way to winning the game. Gar seethed at the side of the table, his knuckles turning white as he gripped his pool cue.

Dale made his way to the other side of the table, calling out, "Rack 'em up," as he did so.

The gangbanger grabbed the triangle but looked at Gar for confirmation.

"What are you, deaf?! Rack 'em up!" Gar shouted at him. He then turned to Dale. "You better not be hustling me, Dale, or you're in the worst trouble of your life."

Dale just shrugged, although inside he was shaking with fear. He hoped Billy would keep the game going so they could get their answers and then get out of there with their lives intact. Or at least Dale's life. Billy was already dead.

When the rack was ready, Dale broke, two balls falling in naturally. And again, with Billy's help, Dale ran the table. It took less than five minutes, and when he sank the eight ball to win the second game and the bet, he jumped up. "Yes!" he shouted.

But his joy was short-lived when he heard the snap of a pool cue being broken in half. "Get that mother!" Gar shouted. And various gangbangers moved toward Dale from the front and behind.

"Swing your cue behind you!" Billy shouted in Dale's ear.

"What?" Dale shouted back, unsure what to do.

"I said swing your cue, or you're a dead man."

Dale froze, watching the gang members move toward him as if in slow motion.

He heard Billy shout, "Dammit!"

The rest of the action was a blur. Dale felt his body twisting and turning, felt the pool cue in his hand swinging left and right, connecting with heads and knees. He felt his fist moving quickly back and forth, then pain when his knuckles split as he hit flesh and bone. He saw gangbangers fall on their asses without anyone touching them. And then he saw Gar leap across the table, and at the same time, his own hands grabbed a ball from the nearest pocket and threw it at Gar.

The ball connected dead center on Gar's forehead and knocked him back, stunning him for a second. But he shook off the blow and started to move forward, only to be hit in the same spot by another ball Dale threw. This time Gar reacted as if he was shot in the head. He landed flat on his back on the pool table, his head hitting the green felt with a hard thump.

Dale felt himself jump up onto the table and then straddle Gar, pinning the gangbanger's arms to his side with his knees.

Then Dale felt his right hand moving to Gar's belt, undoing a clip at the side and pulling out a long, serrated knife. His hand moved and held the knife at Gar's throat. Dale felt his hand move to cut into the skin, but he fought it.

"No, Billy, don't do it!" Dale shouted. "We need to ask him some questions first."

Dale fought Billy for control of his hand for a few more seconds. Then his hand was given back to him along with the rest of his body. He slumped forward in pain, his split knuckles and all his muscles in agony because at no time in his life had he moved so quickly and hit so hard.

Dale knew he had to keep himself together, lest Gar and his gang regain their strength. But then Dale looked around him and saw six or so gangbangers on the floor moaning in pain, and Gar was staring up at him with a look of shock and awe.

The rest of the crowd had the same expression on their faces, and Dale realized that he must look pretty badass as he sat astride Gar holding a knife to the gang leader's neck. A big smile spread across his face as it dawned on him that no matter what he did in his life, even if he did a whole bunch of stupid and idiotic things, he would be remembered as the dude who took out Gar and his gang with his bare fists, a pool cue and a couple of pool balls. He knew it wasn't a story he had to tell anyone; it would be told throughout the Rez over and over again.

"Holy crap, what the heck did you do?" Dale asked Billy.

Gar thought Dale was talking to him so he began to stammer, "I, I, did nothing. It was all their fault."

"Shut up! I wasn't talking to you!" Dale shouted at Gar. He tapped his earpiece. "I was talking to one of my ladies on my phone. She spilled some beer on my carpet." Dale knew it was a lie, but he was in the zone. After this, no one would doubt anything he said, even if it was the biggest lie in the world.

"Sorry, baby, I got interrupted. So tell me again, what the heck did you do?"

"Don't push it, Dale," Billy said. "Start asking him questions, and let's get out of here."

"Are you kidding me? This is totally awesome. Tell me what you did."

"I have no idea. I saw what was going to happen, and I had to do something. I didn't think; I just reacted. Maybe it had something to do with the Steven Seagal movie I saw a couple of days before I died."

"Whatever, it's totally cool," Dale said, still excited. "So what happens now?"

"Start asking him questions. If he killed me, you can take him in."

"Okee-dokee."

Dale then lowered his voice an octave. "Okay, baby, you clean that stuff up, and I'll be home soon to take care of your needs."

"Jeez, Dale, can we move this forward a smidge?"

"You got it, baby, kiss kiss." Dale turned his attention to Gar, trying to look as badass as possible. Gar's face was still contorted in fear but with a twinge of confusion, too. His whole life had collapsed around him, and now it was becoming more surreal by the minute.

"Okay, Gar. I'm going to take it easy on you. I'm just going to ask you a few questions, and then we'll forget all of this ever happened so we can move on with our lives." Dale knew both of their lives would be changed by this event; his for the better, Gar's for the worse.

"Yeah, whatever you want, Dale. Whatever you want."

"Okay, the first question I want you to answer is this…" he paused for effect. "What's the square root of 3489?"

"Square root of what?" Gar said, becoming even more confused and afraid.

"Come on, Dale, don't be a dick about this," Billy said. "Just ask him if he killed me."

"Okay, okay. I'm only having a bit of fun. I don't really want to know the square root of 3489. What I really want to know is if you killed Billy."

"What!? Kill Billy? What the heck are you talking about?" Gar exclaimed.

"It's simple. Did you kill Billy or not? Did you shoot him in the head?"

"Billy was shot in the head?" Gar shouted, his eyes wide. "When did that happen?"

"Nobody knows when it happened, but someone shot him in the head and left him for dead at Twin Bridges."

"And you think I did it?"

"Your gang has access to the kind of gun that killed Billy so, logically, I thought it was you."

"Well, I didn't do it. I didn't even know he was dead."

Dale raised the knife from Gar's neck, and the gang leader sighed with relief. The injured members of his gang started to regain their senses, but the ones who managed to get back to their feet weren't going to take the chance of attacking Dale again.

"You think he's lying?" Dale asked Billy.

"I'm not lying," Gar said. "I didn't kill Billy."

"I don't know. Doesn't look like he's lying. He's pretty scared," Billy said.

"So what now? If Gar didn't do it, who did?" Dale hadn't noticed he was waving the knife around as he spoke.

But Gar did. He watched every single movement of the knife with fearful eyes. "I don't know," Gar said, beginning to sob. "I don't know."

"Wait a second," Billy said. "It's true that Gar's gang has access to the kind of gun that killed me, but maybe he sold the gun to somebody. And that person, for whatever reason, used it to kill me. Ask him if he sold a gun and to whom."

So Dale did. And the answer Gar gave surprised almost everyone.

Twenty-one

Dale slept in his truck, which he had parked across the road from the oil company. And despite the plush seats, he was still uncomfortable. People were meant to sleep lying down, not sitting up. Dale also realized how much he missed his quilt. Without it, he spent a cold night, even though it was summer. His sleep was fitful, broken up into chops and chunks. He could have returned to Aunt Kena's house, but he never liked sleeping there. Her spare bed was lumpy, and the house always had too many unexplained noises. And since Dale wanted to be around when the oil company office opened, going back to his own place in the city was also out of the question.

When he awoke a final time, he was in great physical pain. Not only were his neck and shoulders stiff from the position he had slept in, but every muscle in his body cried out in agony. He had never felt such pain in his life, and for a moment, he thought he was having some kind of attack.

"Good God," he said out loud. "I think I'm going to die."

"You'll be fine," Billy said. "You're just not used to it."

Dale couldn't see Billy; he was still a flicker of light in the seat next to him, like a weird kind of Tinker Bell. But Dale could hear him clearly in his earpiece.

"Of course I'm not used to this. I never sleep in my truck. I usually sleep in my comfy king-size bed with my thick quilt and my ergonomic pillow."

"I'm not talking about the truck, I'm talking about what happened last night. Your body is completely out of shape. You probably pulled every muscle in your body doing all that fighting last night."

"I didn't do any fighting; that was all you. How come I have to suffer the consequences of your actions?"

"My actions but your body. And don't worry about it. The pain will go away, but the reputation of you as a kick-ass ass kicker will never fade. No one's going to mess with you. Ever."

Dale smiled brightly, remembering the expression on everyone's faces after he battled Gar and his gang. And the stunned looks as he jumped off the pool table to leave the bar. Dale couldn't help himself and had to add something extra. He had grabbed the triangle from the floor and tossed it onto the table next to the prone Gar.

"Rack 'em up, boys," Dale had shouted. "This game is over."

Admittedly, it wasn't much, but it was the best Dale could have said. He didn't play pool that much so he wasn't up on the vernacular of the sport. Still, he felt it was cool enough.

And he knew Billy was right. After last night, nobody was going to mess with him. He just wished it didn't hurt so much. None of the action heroes in the movies were in pain after taking on a bunch of guys. Then again, most of the action heroes probably had stunt doubles doing their fighting.

Dale didn't get to think about the fight anymore because at just that second, Grant's truck pulled into the parking lot. He parked in his spot in front of the company's office and slowly got out.

As soon as he saw him, Dale didn't like him. Grant was thin and stylish, with horn-rimmed glasses and one of those cool haircuts all the hipsters in the city always sported, updos that didn't look like an updo. He was also slightly tanned. *Probably does fakinbake*, Dale thought to himself.

Dale quickly started the engine and gunned into the parking lot while Grant was trying to unlock the office door.

Grant turned at the sound of the roaring engine and saw the truck coming toward him. His eyes opened wide with fear when he saw the truck. He worked faster to open the locked door, but in his panicked state he became clumsy. The brakes on the truck screeched as Dale jammed on the pedal. He didn't know why Grant was afraid, but he didn't want the oil company exec to get away. Dale tried to jump out of the truck, but he forgot he was wearing his seatbelt and almost choked himself. He cursed and fiddled with the belt to release it, but his arm muscles hurt so much that he could barely control them. So in the same way that Grant fumbled with his keys, Dale fumbled with his seatbelt.

Dale finally got his seatbelt off at the same instant that Grant unlocked the office door. Grant yanked the door open and tried to quickly shut it, but the automatic door mechanism prevented it from slamming. No matter how hard Grant tried to slam the door, it would only close at its own slow-motion pace.

It was the opening Dale needed. He jumped out of the truck, but as soon as he put one foot on the ground, the truck started to roll forward, with Dale twisting half of his body in the moving truck and the other half on the ground. He had forgotten to put the truck in park.

So somehow, and even though his whole body screamed in pain, he managed to hop back into the truck, step on the brake and put the gear into park so the truck wouldn't crash through the office window.

By the time Dale got the truck in park and jumped out, ready to take down the company man, Grant had locked the front door and disappeared into the back.

Dale punched the office window in anger and frustration at being so close. Pain flashed into his fist and up into his arm and down his shoulder and back. He hopped around, cursing and holding his injured hand.

He shook off the pain and anger and tried to calm himself. After taking a few breaths, he spoke to Billy, "Can you open the door?" It was a great idea, he thought. Billy had figured out how to control pool balls and make Dale fight like Jackie Chan, so opening a locked door should be a piece of cake.

Dale waited for a few seconds before the bolt on the inside of the door clicked. He swung the door open. A chime sounded as he walked in.

Grant peeked around the door of his office. When he saw Dale, he yelped and jumped back quickly. He slammed his office door, the lock clicking into place.

Dale ran down the hallway, and thinking that he could easily break down Grant's door, threw his shoulder into it like he was body checking someone in hockey. Unfortunately, the door gave only slightly and then snapped into place, flinging Dale onto his ass. He bounced so hard on the floor that his ball cap flew off his head.

Billy sighed. Dale shook off his fall and sheepishly got back to his feet. He slowly picked up his cap, brushed it off and put it on his head.

"Sorry. Could you please open the door, Billy?"

"Sure, but watch yourself. Grant might be carrying the gun that Gar said he dropped off here the other day," Billy said. "I don't think he'll shoot you right here because that would give everything away, but you can't be too careful."

Dale froze as he heard Grant's door unlock. Gar told him that he had received a phone call a few days ago asking Gar to drop off a gun in a plain, brown package addressed to Grant and marked *Confidential*. This would ensure that the receptionist wouldn't open the package and would just place it on Grant's desk for him to open.

As soon as Billy unlocked the door, Dale heard scuffling on the other side. He slowly moved forward, afraid that Grant was reaching for the gun and was preparing to shoot.

Billy spoke into Dale's ear. "Don't worry. He doesn't have a gun, I checked. He's just trying to escape out the window, but I locked it. He's trapped."

Dale still didn't want to move. But he felt something push him forward. He stumbled and burst through the office door, barely stopping himself from falling onto the floor.

What Billy said was true: Grant was wrestling with the window locks. He was holding the handle with both hands and had one leg up on the narrow ledge trying to force the window open. He turned quickly at Dale's entrance and set his foot back down on the floor. Grant pressed his back against the wall, seemingly trying to get as far away as he could from Dale in the small space. His eyes blinked quickly and his breathing was shallow. He seemed like a mouse cornered by a cat, and Dale realized he, Dale, was the cat.

Dale was enjoying the feeling of having people being afraid of him, even supposed killers like Grant. And Gar. Especially Gar. Dale figured he would have to do something special with this new power and reputation he had gained. Become some sort of avenging angel or a private detective hired by the poor and weak to protect them from evil. He thought it was a great idea. If he managed to catch the person who murdered Billy, without getting himself killed, he'd open up the Rez's first detective agency. He probably wouldn't make much money, but being a tough private dick was cooler than doing IT in the city.

Dale sauntered into the room, taking his time and letting Grant sweat with fear. "Do you know who I am?" he asked quietly.

"Yeah, yeah, you're Dale," Grant said, his breathing short and sharp. "You're the guy who took out Gar and his boys."

Dale sat on the edge of Grant's desk. "Oh, you heard about that, huh?"

"Everyone has. It's the talk of the Rez. Even some folks in the city who have ties to the Rez are talking about it."

"Well, it's good to know that my reputation precedes me," Dale said, still using a quiet tone. "Do you know why I'm here?"

Grant shook his head. "I have no idea. We've never met before."

"Then how do you know my name is Dale, and why did you run when you saw me?"

"Gar told me about you. He called me on my cell when I was driving here and said someone named Dale might be coming to pay me a visit. He didn't say why; he just said you would, and he told me to watch myself because you were surprisingly fast and mean. Said you took out a bunch of his boys. He sounded scared, and it takes a lot to scare Gar."

"Ahh, Gar. I'm glad he remembered our encounter last night. It wasn't as pleasant as I hoped."

"Can we get on with this," Billy said in Dale's ear-piece. "There's no need for stretching this out. Just ask him if he killed me, and then take him in. He scared shitless of you so he'll go without putting up a fight."

Dale shook his head and waved his hand. Grant looked at Dale, confused, yet still fearful. "So did Gar tell you why I was coming?" Dale asked.

"No, he didn't. He just said you were, and that I should be careful."

"And you still came to work? Even with that warning?"

"Gar's a bit of a jerk," Grant said with a weak laugh. "I really don't take him seriously. I mean, I heard what you did, but it didn't make sense to me why you would come looking for me."

Dale made a move, pretending to chew a fingernail and then flicking the piece into the air. "I'm Billy's cousin," he said dramatically.

Grant looked at him, a blank expression on his face. After a second, he asked, "Billy who?"

"Billy Ghostkeeper."

Again, a look of confusion. And then Grant's eyes lit up with recognition. "Oh, Billy, the guy who works with Matt over at the compliance office. Yeah, I know Billy. Good guy. You're his cousin? Wow, I don't see the resemblance. How is Billy?"

Now it was Dale's turn to be confused. This was not going as well as he had hoped. Grant was supposed to collapse in guilt and beg for mercy. And then Dale was supposed to take him in and become the hero. He wasn't expecting this. He even heard an intake of breath from Billy at Grant's reaction.

"Billy is dead," Dale said. "Didn't you know that?"

Grant's face fell with shock. "Billy's dead? When did that happen?"

"I found his body yesterday."

Grant slowly moved away from the wall and dropped down into his chair, stunned. "Oh, my god, that's horrible." He looked up at Dale. "That must have been awful for you."

"Yeah, it was," Dale said, the image of Billy's body laying on the ground coming back to him. All the bravado that he was projecting simply disappeared. He was no action hero; he was just a dude who did IT in the city and came to help his old aunt on the Rez once in a while, and he had not only discovered that his cousin was dead, but he had also found the body. He shuddered at the memory.

"How did he die? Was he sick? I didn't know he was sick. He didn't look sick the last time I saw him."

Dale looked at Grant with incredulity. "You don't know how he died?"

Grant shook his head.

"But you shot him," Dale said. "You shot him in the head, didn't you?"

Grant's face took on a deeper look of honest shock. Even so, he managed to shake his head.

Twenty-two

Dale looked at Grant with amazement. "You didn't kill Billy?"

Grant shook his head again. "No, I didn't kill Billy."

"He's lying," Billy said. "He killed me."

"He's lying?" said Dale.

"I'm not lying," Grant said, thinking Dale was talking to him.

"He says he's not lying," Dale said.

"I'm not lying," Grant said.

"He is lying. He killed me."

"He's lying?" Dale repeated.

"He's not...I mean...I'm not lying," Grant said.

"He is lying," replied Billy.

"Stop, stop, stop!" Dale shouted, waving his hands in the air. He was tired, his body ached and he was grumpy and hungry. All he wanted to do was go home and crash for several hours. This was not the way he had expected to spend his few days off.

"But I didn't kill him," Grant pleaded.

"I said stop!" Dale shouted, causing the oilman to flinch in his chair.

"You can't trust him…" Billy started.

"Shut up!" Dale shouted, again causing Grant to flinch.

"But I didn't…" Grant started to say.

"Jeez, doesn't anyone understand the concept of 'Shut up'?" Dale pointed at Grant. "You, shut up." And then he pulled his Bluetooth off his ear. "And you, too." He shoved the earpiece into his pocket. "I need to think, and no one, and I mean no one, should talk to me unless I speak first."

Dale was not only grumpy and tired, but he was confused as well. The whole point of breaking into Grant's office and threatening him was to get him to confess to killing Billy. But Grant didn't confess; he said he didn't even know Billy was dead. So if Grant didn't kill Billy, who did?

"Okay, Grant, you say that you didn't kill Billy, but you could be lying," Dale said, pointing an accusing finger at the company man. "Why should I believe you?"

"Because I didn't do it. I didn't even know he was dead. And why would I kill Billy, anyway? I liked him."

"That's no excuse. People kill people they like all the time. You killed Billy because he had information that would bring the company down, and you had to do something to stop him."

"Bring the company down? How could Billy bring down a multinational corporation worth over three hundred billion dollars?"

"He knew you guys were fudging your emission and water sample numbers, hiding the fact the emissions were causing the deaths of some people on the Rez."

"What? There's no proof of that."

"Billy had proof, and he was going to blow the whistle on the company. He was going to go public with the information, and that would ruin the company's reputation and force the government to shut down all your operations on the Rez."

"Are you serious?" Grant said with a little laugh. "Is that what you think is going on?"

"Of course. Why else would you kill Billy?"

"For one thing, I didn't kill Billy. And for another, even if we did fudge the numbers and as a result hide the fact the emissions may have caused the death of a couple kids, and I'm not saying that's what happened, I'm only speaking hypothetically. But even if that all happened, there is no way the government would shut down our operations and bring the company down. They couldn't afford to do that. Do you know how many jobs and tax dollars they would lose? Look at the BP oil spill in the Gulf of Mexico. That caused untold damage, decimating an entire ecosystem, and the explosion that caused the spill killed eleven people. No one shut down BP. The *Exxon Valdez* was one of the worse oil spills on record, but Exxon is still going. Hell, Union Carbide killed almost three thousand people in India, and the only thing they had to do was pay an out-of-court settlement. Not only is that company still highly profitable, but they're also fighting whether they should clean up the plant that killed all those people.

"So there's no way any government is going to shut us down based on information from a lowly employee like Billy."

Dale knew that Billy was upset about Grant's last comment because a glass paperweight flew off Grant's desk and fell to the floor. Dale resisted the temptation to put the Bluetooth in his ear. He didn't feel like listening to Billy's ranting.

"I thought you said you liked Billy?" Dale asked.

"I did. He was a good guy, and I'm really sorry to hear he's gone. But that doesn't mean I should lie about him. He wasn't a big wheel or anything. He was just an assistant compliance officer with the band. And there are tons of guys like him doing the same job. He can easily be replaced. In fact… I'll offer you Billy's old job. Good pay, lots of benefits."

"I don't want Billy's job," Dale said with indignation. "I already have a job in the city. Besides, Billy has just died, and it would be ghoulish for me to take his job so soon."

"Oh, come on," Grant said, his confidence returning. "It's not like you'd be sleeping with his wife. It's just business. And business for DBA Resources is a 24/7 operation; it stops for no one and nothing. This entire Rez could die tonight of some terrible affliction, me included, and business wouldn't stop. It would just keep on going because that's what it does."

"That's just sick."

"That's just business."

Dale suddenly remembered what Gar had told him, and he knew he had Grant now. "But what about Gar and the gun?"

"Gar and the gun?" Grant asked. "What about Gar, and what gun?"

"Gar said he delivered a gun to you."

"Gar said he sent me a gun?"

"That's what he said."

"He said that?"

"Will you stop doing that!" Dale shouted. "Gar told me last night that he got a call from someone, he assumed it was you, and that person told him to drop off a gun at the office."

"So Gar dropped off a gun at the office? Just like that?"

"No, he said he put it in a package confidentially addressed to you. That's why he assumed it was you who had called him."

"And you believe Gar?"

"Of course I do. I had just taken out six of his guys, and I was sitting on his chest waving a knife in his face when he told me. He was telling me the truth."

"Yeah, he probably was. Gar comes across as tough, but he's really a coward, which is why I don't like using him that much."

"Wait. What do you mean you don't like *using him that much?* Why would an oil company want to use a bunch of gangbangers like him?"

Grant shrugged. "We like to carry out geological tests on certain sections of land, but there are rare situations when a landowner refuses access, so we send over Gar and a few of his boys to convince the landowner that it's in his best interest to work with us instead of against us."

"The company uses Gar as muscle?" Dale said, his eyes wide with shock. "That's unconscionable, that's, that's…" he stammered.

"That's business," Grant said plainly. "And the natural resource business is highly competitive. You need to use all your wits, all the skill sets and resources in your basket in order to succeed and destroy your competitors. Only the grocery industry is more competitive than the resource industry. I'm tough, but compared to those grocery guys, I'm a cute little pussycat."

"So is it part of the business to commit murder?"

"No, of course not," Grant said, acting insulted. "Who do you think we are, the mafia?"

"You guys are worse. You pass yourself off as good corporate citizens while at the same time causing damage to the environment and the deaths of thousands of people."

"I didn't say we did that kind of stuff. I was just giving you some examples of how the world works. You are really naïve about this kind of stuff."

"Shut up!" Dale said, raising his hand as if to strike. Grant flinched, cowering behind his raised hands. All Grant's confidence was suddenly gone in a second. Dale enjoyed this new power of his. Especially holding it over a jerk like Grant.

But he had to be careful or he would turn into someone like Grant. Or worse, like Gar.

"It's got nothing to do with naiveté; it's just being a decent person and believing that everyone else wants to be decent as well," Dale said. "Guys like you make me sick. You've always made me sick, thinking you're doing good when you're actually assholes. And then when you're called on it, you say crap like 'that's way the world works' or 'at least we're not as bad as some other criminals.' And that makes you worse because those criminals know they're criminals. You guys think that if it weren't for you, the world would collapse. And maybe it would, but at least we'd get a chance to build a better one without you."

Another paperweight fell to the floor; Billy telling him something, probably to take it easy and get the information. So Dale pulled back his hand, and caught his breath.

"So, Grant," he said.

"Please don't hurt me," Grant said, still cowering.

"I'm not going to hurt you. I just want information."

"I don't have any information."

"Sure you do. Tell me why Gar delivered a gun to you."

"I don't know why he sent me a gun."

"Ahh, so you admit that he sent you a gun." Dale said, snapping his fingers.

"It's possible. I have no idea."

"Okay, if it's possible he sent you a gun, then it's possible you killed Billy. I mean, I'm not saying you did," Dale said, thinking that maybe it was time to play the good cop instead of a bad one, even though he wasn't really a cop. "I'm just saying that because Gar sent you the gun, it begs the question, why? Why would he send you a gun? That is the type of question people are going to ask. And that question may lead some people, like the police, to believe that you did kill Billy, which would be bad for you. And *just* you, not the company. Not DBA Resources."

"But I didn't kill Billy," Grant said.

"I'm not saying you did. I'm just saying because the gun was sent to you, people will speculate that you did."

"But there's no way that I could have killed Billy be… because I was out of town all week," Grant said with a stammer in his voice. "I…I was in Mexico on vacation so it makes no difference whether people think that Gar sent me a gun because I wasn't here to accept it. I just got back last night."

Dale held up his finger and opened his mouth for a rebuttal, but he could think of nothing in response. And he didn't have to put the Bluetooth back on because he knew that Billy was just as tongue-tied as he was.

Twenty-three

Dale left Grant sitting in his office, and he drove to Aunt Kena's house. He put the Bluetooth in his ear, but he had nothing to say to Billy.

Despite all their work, all the pain, the cousins had drawn a big fat zero. Even though he hadn't originally believed Grant when he denied killing Billy, Dale had no choice but to believe him in the end. Grant had been on his way home from Mexico when Billy was shot. So there was no way he could have killed him.

But Dale still believed Grant was somehow involved in the murder; he just couldn't figure out how. There had to be something else, but Dale was drawing a blank. He wasn't qualified for this kind of stuff. He felt like he was letting Billy down by not figuring out who killed him and why.

"Well, that was some speech," Billy said. "Completely unexpected but still a solid speech. You've done good, Dale."

"Nah, I did nothing. I didn't solve anything. I let you down, Billy, and I'm sorry."

"Let me down? Are you crazy? You did a lot more than I expected you to. You found my body, which I know wasn't pleasant, and then you called the cops. You handled an interrogation by the cops so well that they let you go when they should have taken you in. And not only that, you stood up to Gar."

"That wasn't me. That was all you taking on Gar and his dudes. If it wasn't for you, I'd be dead in another ditch somewhere."

"I'm not talking about the fight and all that. I'm talking about what *you* did. You could have said no when I asked you to go into that bar and confront Gar, and no one, not even I, would have blamed you if you had said no because of what Gar did to you in high school. In fact, I had no right to ask you to do that, knowing what Gar did to you back then. But you went in anyway. You did, not knowing if I could help you. You knew that if you went into the bar and faced Gar, something bad would happen to you, but you went in anyway. That took a lot of guts."

"It was nothing. I knew you would make something happen. I knew you would figure out a way to help me somehow."

"No, you didn't, so stop lying," Billy said. "And stop saying that you let me down when everything you've done in the last day or so has been just the opposite. I'm the one who let you down. I'm the one who let those two kids die, and I'm the one who asked you to go into the bar when I knew you would get hurt. And you know what? I'm also the one who should have been checking on Aunt Kena every week, bringing her food and dealing with her craziness instead of you. You live in the city, and I know it takes at least half a day of your time to do that. I lived only a few minutes away from her, but I always thought I was too busy or too important to help her.

"You're the one that did all the good and right things here, Dale. Just like any good guy should," Billy said, his voice cracking. "I didn't, and I'm a dead jerk because of it. I'm sorry."

Dale was at a loss for words. His family was slightly crazy, and they weren't the kind of people to admit they had done something wrong and apologize for it. He appreciated what his cousin said, but he also still felt things were not complete and it was because of him.

He was going to Aunt Kena's house because that was where this whole situation started, and he figured that if he went back there, everything would begin to make sense. Even though it was a crazy place. But as he drove and looked out his window, one question popped into his mind.

"What's with the bird?" he said, gesturing to the crow who was sitting on the truck's side mirror, with none of its feathers ruffling even though Dale was doing eighty clicks an hour. He knew the bird had to be important because it followed him everywhere. The crow had been outside Aunt Kena's when this whole mess had all started; it had guided Dale to Twin Bridges where he found Billy's body; the bird had waited on a fence wire outside of the bar and the company's office; and now it was sitting on the mirror calmly preening itself with not a care in the world.

"Oh, that," Billy said with a sigh. "That's my spirit guide. Or at least someone who claims to be my spirit guide."

"Really? That's cool. I always wanted a spirit guide."

"It's not all it's cracked up to be. Trust me."

Dale tapped on the side window, trying to get the bird's attention. "Hey, birdie. Birdie, birdie, birdie," he said in a high-pitched voice. "Come on, birdie."

"I don't think he's going to like that."

"Sure it will. Come on, it's a bird," Dale said, tapping the window again. He raised his voice to a higher pitch. "Aren't you, birdie, birdie? You're kind of an ugly bird, but you're still cute. Aren't you, cute birdie?"

The crow turned and seemed to frown at Dale with distaste. Then it spread its wings and allowed the air to lift it up away from the truck.

"Awww. Come on back, birdie." Dale looked to the left and right to see if he could find the bird. He looked in the side mirrors but couldn't see the crow. But he did spot a truck behind him, flashing its lights. And he also heard the constant beeping of a horn. At first he thought it was Gar and his boys, coming after him for revenge. But then Dale realized that Gar wasn't stupid enough to flash his lights and beep his horn.

Dale slowed and allowed the truck to catch up. He pulled over to the side of the road, stopped and opened his side window. The other truck pulled alongside him, and the driver rolled down the passenger window.

In the driver's seat was Matt, Billy's co-worker. Dale had met him many times; he knew Matt's younger brother when they were in a computer club in high school.

"Thank God I caught up with you, Dale," Matt said, smiling brightly. "I've been trying to find you all last night and today."

"What's up, Matt?"

"I heard that you were checking around to try to figure out who killed Billy."

"Yeah, what about it."

"I also heard you talked to Grant."

"Yeah, I did…" Dale was going to say that Grant wasn't very helpful. But Matt didn't let him finish.

"Well, everything Grant said was probably a lie; he's that kind of guy."

Dale did a mental fist bump. "I knew it. He was lying about something. The guy's a big weasel."

"You have no idea. But I know exactly what's going on, and I have some information that will explain everything."

Yes! This case isn't dead yet, Dale thought. It was the break he and Billy were looking for. "Excellent, Matt. What you got?"

"I gotta show you. Come on, get in my truck." Matt reached across his seat and flung the passenger door open.

"Nah, I'll just follow you. I don't want to leave my truck here."

"It'll be fine, this is the Rez. Come on, it'll be faster if you come with me. That way if I make some quick turns, I won't lose you. Time is of the essence here."

Dale jumped out of his truck and dashed across to Matt's. He climbed into the passenger seat and slammed the door. "All right, let's go," he said excitedly.

Matt nodded and gunned his truck forward.

When Dale jumped out of his truck, Billy had gotten out as well. Billy wanted to get into Matt's truck, to ride in the box, but when he tried, some kind of force stopped him. He didn't know what it was, but it felt evil. He tried again, and this time, whatever it was, was much strong than he was. It pushed him back, knocking him to the ground. The pain in his head returned, and Billy finally realized who had killed him.

Matt's truck sped down the road, gravel flying from the spinning rear tires.

The crow was perched on a nearby telephone pole and looked down at Billy. "That's not good," he said without any emotion.

Twenty-four

Billy felt a bit woozy for a second. His vision faded in and out. He seemed to be at work, sitting at his desk. After a moment of disconnection, Billy felt comfortable in his body again. But he felt detached, almost as though he was watching himself. It was like remembering something but feeling like you were actually right there, experiencing it in the flesh again. But that feeling faded, replaced by a sensation of righteous justice.

He had finally decided to do something about all the figures he had been hiding. To finally pass the information on to the government ministry that oversaw the resource companies. He would make sure the Jennings kids had not died in vain.

He had spent several days writing his report, compiling the numbers, organizing it into a coherent package so they would take him seriously and not see him as some crazy person filled with hyperbole or that had an axe to grind.

Matt had been watching him closely, and Billy knew his supervisor was suspicious of all the work he was doing. But Billy said nothing, knowing Matt would probably try to talk him out of submitting the report. Billy had tried to talk himself out of it many times as well. He weighed the pros and cons over and over again, losing a lot of sleep in the process. He knew he would lose his job, knew Matt would probably lose his job too, along with some others. He knew the company would be in trouble. But in the end, he couldn't bear the thought that the two Jennings kids had died and he might have been able to prevent their deaths.

But once he completed the report and sent it off, he knew he had to tell Matt. When he finally went to Matt's office and told him what he'd done, Matt didn't interrupt him, didn't chastise him, didn't even flinch when Billy started tearing up as he talked about the Jennings kids. Matt listened carefully, nodded when he was supposed to and handed Billy a tissue to dry his tears.

And when Billy finished talking, Matt just leaned back in his chair, took a couple of deep breaths and rubbed his face and head with his hands. He said nothing for about a minute, his face pensive, almost on the verge of some kind of emotional response, but he held it in.

"Okaaaay," Matt said, exhaling the word rather than saying it. "First, I wish you would have talked to me about this before you sent in the report." Matt's tone wasn't angry; he seemed a little disappointed but not much.

"You would have just talked me out of it."

"Yeah, I would have, because this has a lot of implications you might not be aware of."

"I know that. This wasn't easy for me to do. And I really thought about the implications for a long time, but in the end, I figured that something had to be done. We can't go on like this." For some strange reason, Billy felt like he was breaking up with someone.

"Yeah, I guess. But there are even more implications you don't know about. This isn't going to be easy."

"I know that. I haven't slept in a week, and I probably won't get a good night's sleep for a long time."

Matt sighed deeply and rubbed his face again. Billy knew that Matt was thinking about his kids and his family, wondering how he would explain why Daddy didn't have a job anymore. Billy also knew Matt was thinking how he would explain the situation to Grant. The company would not be pleased and would probably fight these allegations to the end. They wouldn't take the report sitting down. And Matt would be in the middle of everything.

Billy wished he could make things easier for Matt, but he just couldn't see a way.

After a few more minutes, Matt jumped out of his chair, shaking his hands as if they had fallen asleep. He paced for a minute or so. "You know what, I can't think in here. I need to get outside," he said. "I need to go somewhere quiet and figure out what to do next."

"Sure, Matt, you do what you need to do," Billy said. "I'm sorry I sprang this on you at the last minute, but I had to do what I thought was best for those two kids and the other families in the area."

"Yeah, for the kids," Matt said, distractedly. He stood still for a moment, then grabbed his keys off his desk and headed for the door. Before he stepped out, he turned back to Billy. "You wanna come with me? I mean, we don't have to talk about anything, but I just don't think I should be alone right now. It's a nice day, and I think it would be good for you to get outside too. We could get something to drink, beers for me, some soda for you, and hang out somewhere, maybe Twin Bridges or something. It's really nice out there."

It is *a nice day,* Billy thought. He realized that the weather over the past week had been warm, and he had missed most of it worrying about work and that report. And Matt was right; Twin Bridges was the perfect place to get away from all the craziness. Quiet, secluded. No one to hassle him. It would be a great break from the stress he was feeling.

"Yeah, that's a great idea. You wanna drive, or what?" replied Billy.

Matt rubbed his face again. "No, you drive yourself out. I'll pick up the drinks and meet you out there. Dr. Pepper's your favorite, right?"

"Yep. And if they don't have it, root beer is fine, too."

As they left the office, Matt told Judy, the receptionist, that they were heading out to one of the sites for some research and development. That was office code for hanging out away from the office.

Matt and Billy climbed into their respective trucks and went their separate ways. It was warm enough that Billy could have put on the air conditioning while he drove, but he decided to roll down the window instead and hang his arm out the window. It was that kind of day.

And as he drove, he felt the weight of the report and the two Jennings kids lift off his shoulders. He still worried, but he was more convinced he had done the right thing. Talking to Matt helped. And having Matt seem so upbeat and wanting to drive to Twin Bridges to clear their heads was great. It proved to Billy that Matt might even be on his side, that he would support him and join the fight.

And when Billy turned into the Twin Bridges area, parked his truck and walked down into the ravine, he knew getting away from the office had been a good idea. The air was so clean, the stream so clear and the sounds of the wind, the birds and the babbling water so soothing. He imagined living centuries in the past, before the Europeans came and the land was untouched, when the grasslands were all natural, no barley or wheat monoculture, and outside the ravine, ranged thousands upon thousands of buffalo.

He wondered if a guy like him could have survived in that time, but he figured he would have been given the skills to hunt, fish and take care of his people. He wouldn't be the same person he was now if he had been alive back then.

He thought more about that time, about whether he could actually hunt, kill, skin and butcher a large buffalo.

He would love to try it some day, but he'd probably never get the chance. He could dream, couldn't he?

And then he heard a rustling in the trees, someone was coming down the path leading into the ravine.

Billy turned and saw Matt. With his back to the creek, Billy watched as Matt came closer. But Matt wasn't carrying any beers or Dr. Pepper. He was holding something else in his hand, but Billy couldn't see what it was.

"You forgot our drinks," Billy said, jokingly.

But Matt didn't smile. His face was passive but tight, as if he was holding something in. Billy didn't know what to make of it.

Then Matt raised his arm. Billy saw a long barrel pointed at him. It looked like some kind of toy gun. Maybe Matt was planning on a water fight, a bit of fun before he went back to his truck to get the drinks?

Then Billy realized it was not a toy gun. The opening in the barrel looked too large.

"What the heck?" Billy said, shocked that Matt would play this kind of mean joke on him. "Not funny, Matt."

Matt shook his head. And then there was a flash. An instant later, an explosion of noise.

Then nothing. It wasn't like sleep where you dreamt. There was no sense of time, no sense of anything. It was just nothing.

Then Billy woke and had started talking to a crow.

Twenty-five

B illy jerked back to the real world, pulled himself up from his stupor, jumped to his feet and ran after Matt's truck. He could run faster than normal, three times the speed of a live human being in fact. But there was no way he could catch up with the speeding truck.

He knew he wasn't limited to the confines of the physical world, that he could overcome the physics of gravity, time and space. But he only knew that in theory. Putting those ideas and thoughts into practice was another matter. Something deep inside himself was holding him back; it was keeping his feet on the ground and his head in the real world.

So no matter how hard he tried, the band's symbol on the tailgate of Matt's truck got farther and farther away.

Reluctantly, Billy stopped running. He was breathing heavily, and he could feel sweat dripping down his face, even though he knew he was dead and he no longer had to breathe or sweat.

The crow circled around him, squawking. "Don't stop. Keep going. Stop thinking that you're alive. Finally accept that you're dead, or your cousin will soon be joining you."

Billy shut his eyes and tried to center himself. "I'm dead. I'm dead," he said over and over again. He worked to relax his body and to let all thoughts of being alive leave his brain. He tried to calm his breathing so that it would slow his heart rate and relax him. After half a minute, his breathing did slow, as did his heart rate. Then he realized that he was doing it all wrong.

"Stupid!" he shouted at himself. "You're dead. You don't have to worry about your breathing and your heart rate because your lungs and heart don't work anyway."

So Billy focused on not breathing and not having a heartbeat. But that only made him think he was suffocating, which in turn caused his heart to pound even louder in his ears. But he held his breath for as long as he could until he collapsed on the road, panting.

The crow was perched on a fence next to the road, shaking his head and rolling his eyes. "Pathetic," the bird said. "Not only are you the most useless dead person I have ever met, and I've met a lot of dead people, but in all that time you spent holding your breath, Matt has driven your cousin farther down the road. Who knows, by now he could already be dead, and I'll have two idiots to deal with."

For a second, Billy panicked, imagining Dale's ghost showing up and following him for the rest of eternity.

He couldn't decide which would be a worse fate: having Matt kill Dale, or Dale's ghost.

But then Billy realized something: Dale was still alive, at least for now. Matt was taking Dale somewhere secluded to kill him. And Billy knew exactly where.

He grabbed a rock and threw it at the crow. He hit the bird, who fell, stunned, to the road. Billy dashed over and grabbed the bird, wrapping his hands around his small throat.

The crow was still alive but dazed. Billy shook the bird. "Wake up!" he shouted, his face just inches from the bird's head. "Wake up, you stupid bird."

The crow slowly came to. He twisted and struggled, but Billy only squeezed tighter. The bird tried to peck at Billy's hands but Billy squeezed even harder, not trying to kill the bird but just showing who was in control.

The bird stopped struggling and pecking, his dark eyes almost popping out of his head. Billy held the pressure for another second, and then he relaxed his grip.

Instantly, the bird started yelling at him. "How dare you manhandle me! Don't you know who and what you are dealing with? Don't you know the consequences of what you are doing treating me like this. I am no mere bird, I'm one of the seven original…"

Billy squeezed the bird's throat harder, cutting off the tirade. "Shut up, you stupid bird!" he shouted. "There's nothing worse you can do to me now. I'm already dead. So you'd better listen to me, or I'll go all Ozzy Osbourne on your head."

The bird gave Billy a sage nod when he finally released his grip. "Excellent. And now that you've completely accepted your death, you should no longer be bound by the physicality of this world. You should have no trouble catching up to Matt and your cousin."

Billy realized that he could go anywhere he wanted to in this world. And that he could move into the next. Everything around him faded into translucent. The sun in the sky offered him no heat, but he was no longer cold. He could see stars in the daytime. The wind blew over the landscape, but he didn't feel the breeze. He was at the same time standing on the ground and floating above it. A light shone through a hole in the sky; it opened wider, the edges rippling, sparkling. The hole reached down to him or he moved up to it; Billy couldn't tell which. Looking through the hole, he saw an endless prairie, not the golden prairie of fall but the bright green prairie of summer. Hills rolled and undulated into the distance. Along several of these hills, a brown wave moved back and forth. It took him a second to realize that the brown wave was a massive herd of buffalo, running across the prairie. He watched the undulating movement for an endless moment of time as buffalo upon buffalo ran past him. And no matter how long he watched, the buffalo didn't stop.

Billy placed his hand through the hole and felt the warm welcoming of the land. It was a sensation he had never felt before on his life on earth. No matter what had occurred or what he had done in the old world, the good, the bad or the indifferent, he felt he completely belonged in this new world.

The face of Mosum passed before him. The old man offered a look of perfect joy to embrace his grandson, but at the same time, a look of sadness that broke Billy's heart. Mosum beckoned Billy to join him.

And Billy almost did. For a brief second, he touched his grandfather's hand and realized that the most terrible thing he had done, turning his back on his people and causing the death of those young children, was forgiven.

But then Billy withdrew his hand and stepped away from the new world.

Even though he knew this world was where he belonged and was welcomed, he knew he wasn't ready. Mosum may have forgiven him, but he hadn't forgiven himself. He had something left to do in the old world, and if he didn't try to fix his mistakes, the feeling would linger with him in the new world.

He shook his head, and all the visions disappeared. The sun shone down with heat and the wind blew around him. The daytime stars vanished, and everything became solid again. The door to the next world was gone.

Billy relaxed his hands and let the crow go. The bird flew for a few seconds to stretch his wings and then landed softly on Billy's shoulder.

"So now what happens?" the crow asked softly.

Billy thought for a moment, knowing the exact spot Matt would take Dale. Getting there wasn't going to be easy. As a dead man, Billy could do nothing to stop Matt from killing Dale.

But Billy had another idea.

Twenty-six

Billy jumped up and started moving. His movements couldn't be called running because he had fully accepted the fact of his death and was now a spirit of some sort. He headed in the opposite direction of where Matt's truck had gone.

The crow circled around him, screeching out his name, but Billy ignored the bird. He kept moving because he knew there wasn't much time left in Dale's life. If he wanted to save his hapless cousin, he had to act quickly.

But the bird flew in front of his face, yelling out his name, making Billy stop. The bird landed on the road in front of him.

"Out of my way, you stupid bird," Billy said, kicking gravel at the crow. "I don't have time for you; I gotta save my cousin."

The flying gravel went through the bird as if the crow wasn't there. "You're going the wrong way, Billy. Your cousin and Matt went the other way. If you want to save him, you have to turn around. And you'll be able to catch up easily now that you've accepted who and what you are."

"You think I don't know that? But what's the point of catching them?"

"You can save Dale. You can stop Matt from doing to him what he did to you."

"How the heck am I going to do that?" Billy shouted impatiently. "Huh, answer me that. How's a dead person going to stop a live person from killing someone? Scare him to death? I don't think so."

Billy flicked his right wrist in the air to dismiss the bird and kept moving. For a brief second, he felt as though he was being pushed through the bird. It seemed that Billy was moving through water. But then that moment passed, and he stumbled as he moved easily through the air once again.

The bird flew beside him, holding pace next to Billy's head, like a remora fish attached to a shark. "So where the heck are you going, Billy? If you can't save your cousin, who will?"

"Why are you doing this to me?" Billy asked. Since he had accepted his death, Billy had no need to breathe so he wasn't physically held back by his surroundings. And though it seemed like he was talking, he was communicating with the bird in some other way, telepathy or something. "Don't you have something better to do?"

"I have a lot of better things to do. Tons. But as I've said before, I'm stuck here helping you. So, explain to me what your plan is."

"Jeez. For a spirit guide you are pretty stupid, aren't you?" Billy said. "It's actually very simple. Before I accepted I was dead, I would have run far and wide to help Dale on my own, not realizing that as a dead man, there was no way I could stop Matt from killing Dale. I'd just be a witness to his death if I followed them.

"So the only way to help Dale is to get a live person to help us," Billy explained.

"How the heck are you going to do that?" the bird demanded. "As you just said, you're dead. Who's going to listen to you?"

Billy stopped moving. In that short period of time, he had crossed through the village of the Rez and had arrived at the opposite end. A hundred feet in front of him was a familiar house, but it was not the place he remembered. When he was alive, and during the time he was dead and still thinking he was still somehow alive, the house looked old and decrepit, bits of siding and roofing falling off, exposing holes like a decaying corpse. All the plants, trees and bushes around the house were dead. And there was no other life—no birdsong, no wind, no rain, nothing.

But now, because Billy had accepted his death, he saw the place for what it truly was. The house was a massive tee-pee. The poles of the teepee were made out of traditional birch wood, but the poles were the biggest Billy had ever seen. They were at least six feet in circumference and almost forty feet high—and they were made from a single tree, not just logs lashed together. The buffalo-hide walls of the teepee were thick, yet soft. And Billy could detect no seams; it was as if the entire covering was made from the skin of a single giant buffalo.

And instead of the dead plants he'd seen in the old world, a plethora of flora surrounded the teepee. Almost every flower, bush and tree in the Cree lexicon of plants flourished within fifty feet of Aunt Kena's home.

The abundance of plants solved the mystery of how Aunt Kena had harvested all the herbs she had used on her people when they were sick. Everyone thought she had some secret supplier. But no one, except the people who lived in, or understood, the spirit world, knew that Aunt Kena's abilities allowed her to walk just outside her door and pick what she needed whenever she wanted.

And instead of having no animal life around her home in the real world, Aunt Kena's house was surrounded by what could only be described as Walt Disney's wet dream of nature. There were thousands of creatures—songbirds, squirrels, chipmunks, skunks, porcupines, rabbits, beavers, bobcats, deer, elk, moose and countless other woodland animals. A small herd of woodland buffalo munched on grass at the edge of the huge teepee.

A small brook babbled through the property, and a family of beavers had built a small dam that created a tiny lake dotted with geese and ducks and other waterfowl. Every so often, Billy saw a flash and then the splash of a jumping fish.

The teepee itself glowed with a soft inner light and hummed with songs and drums of a quiet powwow.

"Holy cow," Billy said, taking it all in and trying to understand the scene before him. He had the same feeling when the hole had opened up in the fabric of the old world and revealed to him the spirit world. It was a welcome feeling that this was the place he belonged. No wonder his auntie was always cranky; she lived in this beautiful place but was still somehow trapped and haunted by the comparably drab, old world.

Billy knew he was truly in the world of the living.

The crow fluttered down and landed on his shoulder. "Sure is something, isn't it?"

"You said it. I had no idea," Billy said.

"No one really does," the crow said. "And those who do, like your aunt, are treated as crazy people when the truth is that everyone else who doesn't see this or isn't aware of this, is crazy."

Billy nodded in agreement, but then he realized that although this was a wonderful place, people did belong in the old world. They deserved to live there for as long as they could, and they could do as they wished, to love or hate, to be happy or sad. To raise and protect children and to respect the earth so that the entire cycle could continue.

The people living in the real world ensured the existence of the spirit world. Any premature and unnecessary damage to the earth or death in the old world could cause irreparable repercussions in the spirit world.

Billy's actions had caused damage in both worlds, and the only way to redeem himself was to prevent further damage from happening. Which is why he had come to Aunt Kena's house.

"So what happens now?" the crow asked.

Billy pointed at the massive teepee. "Only one person can help Dale now. And she lives in that teepee."

"You sure she can help? Or wants to?"

"She has to."

"What about me?" the crow asked. "You know I won't go in there. The creature that lives in there is too powerful. Sometimes too frightening. But I feel I should help."

"Really? Doesn't sound like you."

"Well, I made a big grumpy bear a promise, and when crows make promises, we keep them."

"Okay. If you really want to help. I need you to find Dale and Matt," Billy said.

"And then what?"

"Do what you do best. Annoy the living shit out of them, and do your best to delay Matt for as long as you can."

"It might not be long enough."

"Do what you can," Billy said. "Even though you've annoyed me, I know you've barely touched the depth of your annoyingness."

"I don't think 'annoyingness' is a real word," the crow chirped sarcastically.

"See, that's the idea," Billy said, batting at the bird to get him off his shoulder. "Now get out of here and delay Dale's murder."

The crow flew in a circle around Billy for a bit. "And what about you? Do you really think she's going to break out of her funk and help save Dale?"

"She'll have to," Billy said. "Because if she doesn't, I'm going to haunt her till the end of time. And if you think you're annoying, you haven't seen how annoying a pissed off Indian can be."

"You sound like your grandfather," the crow said.

"Shut up. And get out of here."

The bird laughed and flew toward Dale and Matt. "Just like your grandfather," he muttered.

Twenty-seven

Billy dashed forward, pushed open the flap and entered the teepee. Surprisingly, the interior looked pretty much the same as Aunt Kena's house normally did. Except next to the TV was a fire pit, the flames licking a hunk of buffalo meat on a traditional, wooden rotisserie. The ghost of the Jennings girl was turning the hand crank.

The girl gave him a shy smile, and Billy felt his heart break once again. A deep sadness came over him, almost forcing him to his knees. But he shook his head and pushed the sadness aside. He replaced it with righteous anger and jumped in front of Aunt Kena, who was sitting in the middle of her couch, eyes glazed, mouth slack, watching the big screen TV that was showing another version of rich, spoiled housewives talking smack to each other.

It took a few moments for Aunt Kena to snap out of her malaise and to realize something was blocking her view. She probably wasn't watching TV but was somewhere else completely.

She squinted her eyes at him, and it was another second before she recognized him. "I thought I told you to knock."

"I'm not a vampire, Aunt Kena," Billy said to her, hands on his hips. "I don't need to knock because I don't need your permission."

"I didn't say it because you need my permission; I just said it to teach you some manners. It's only polite to knock before you enter someone's house."

"I need your help, Aunt Kena."

She made a grunting noise. At first he thought she was choking, and instinctively, he moved forward to help her, even though he could do nothing if she was. But then she started to laugh.

"Take a number, Miss Pîyesî," she said. "I've got so many people from the spirit world asking me for help, I'm thinking of franchising out."

Billy sat to the right of his aunt. On the left was the Jennings boy. The boy was clinging to Aunt Kena's arm, and she either didn't care he was there or she was completely unaware of his presence.

Aunt Kena's didn't look at Billy; she just faded back into her TV show or wherever she had gone. Billy clapped his hands, but she didn't respond. He shouted her name in her ear, but again, she didn't react.

So he grabbed her head, both hands on the side of her head, and turned her to face him. "Aunt Kena!" he shouted. "I need your help."

She looked at him sadly. "It's too late, Miss Pîyesî. It's too late, Billy. You're already dead. I told you that."

"I know, Aunt Kena. I know I'm dead, and I also know why."

Her eyes squinted at him again, and she cocked her head to the side as she gave him a closer once over. "Yes. I see that. You look different. You look ready to go over to the other side. Congratulations. I knew you had it in you."

She made to turn back to the TV, but Billy turned her back again. "No…I mean, yes. I am ready to go over to the other side. But there's one thing I have to fix before I get there."

"Oh, Billy, this world is dead to you," she said sadly. "Forget about it, and move on. Accept your fate, and be at peace. That's the only advice I can give you."

"But what about Dale, Aunt Kena? We have to help Dale."

She shook her head. "Dale's okay. He's a bit of a weirdo and a loser, but it runs in the family. As long as he keeps his nose clean and stays out of trouble, he'll be fine."

"That's what I'm talking about. Dale isn't fine. He's in trouble, and if we don't help him, he'll be dead, just like me. Just like these kids that hang around your place."

Aunt Kena's eyes opened in surprise, but only for a brief moment. Then the look on her face changed to extreme sadness and emptiness. She mumbled something, and Billy thought she said Dale's name. She took a deep breath, and her face returned to her normal look of resigned loss.

"So be it," she said softly.

The little Jennings boy nodded, and Billy heard a voice behind him; the little girl repeated Aunt Kena's words in her soft, tiny voice.

Billy nudged Aunt Kena, knocking her into the little boy. But he knew he couldn't hurt the boy because the kid was already dead. Aunt Kena fell back against the couch, and the boy moved to stand by the TV, out of reach.

"No! Not 'so be it!'" Billy shouted, not just at his aunt but at everyone in the room. "That's what got us in trouble in the first place, saying 'so be it.' That's all we say these days. We see the white man come and take our lands, put our kids in their schools, take away our language and our culture, and we say 'so be it.' We see our kids turn into gangbangers, shooting up our lands and killing themselves and other innocent people, and we say 'so be it.' We see all these corporations, the oil, gas, mining and forestry companies, coming in, bribing our people with shiny beads like useless jobs and money so they can rape our land and leave it empty of animals and trees and impregnate it with a culture of want and fear, and we say 'so be it.'

"And we accept the company's money and promises, and turn our backs on our people, which cause our people, our children, to die of terrible diseases…" Billy's voice broke as he looked at the two Jennings children. Tears flowed down his face as he looked into their eyes, wordlessly asking for their forgiveness. He tried to speak again, but his words caught in his throat as he saw that the two kids had forgiven him for his misdeeds.

"Billy, it's okay," Aunt Kena said, placing her hand on his, sending a wave of soothing warmth into his body, similar to the way alcohol had made him feel but better. This warmth came from his family, from the earth itself. "These things you speak of are only the way of the world. It is how life was, even in the old days of our people. Don't fool yourself into thinking we were great human beings before the Europeans came. We were a good people, yes, but we were human, just like everyone else. If we were so great and wise a people, why did we fail so easily? Why were we so taken in by these Europeans and their promises? This is just how the world is."

Even though it disconnected him from the warmth of his aunt's touch, Billy pulled away. "No. This is not the way of the world. We say it is the way of the world, but we say that because we are too damn lazy. All of us, not just Indians but Europeans, Asians, blacks. We are lazy creatures, us humans, but this is not the way of the world. You have to help me, Aunt Kena. You have to help Dale, and you have to help these children because that's what we do; we help each other."

Aunt Kena smiled but shook her head. "I can't help you. It's too late."

"It's never too late. Sure, we weren't a great people, but we've been on this land for over twenty thousand years, and that has to count for something. Sure, the Europeans have knocked us down, but we're still here. And it has only been a few centuries, which is nothing compared to twenty thousand years. And in another twenty thousand years, we'll still be here. But only if you help. Because if an elder like you can't help us, then it's all lost. Everything. And our twenty thousand years will mean absolutely nothing."

Aunt Kena looked up, her eyes a bit brighter. "You could always speak nice, Billy. That's one reason why I liked you. But I can't help you because I can't help anyone anymore."

"What are you talking about? You're a healer."

"No, I'm not. I let myself get sick. I let myself get the diabetes, and I can't make it go away. What kind of healer lets that happen?"

"The kind of healer that looks after everyone else before they look after themselves. The kind of healer who goes into a sick kid's room when everyone tells her she should stay out so she won't get sick. The kind of healer who stays in that room with that kid for three days, singing to him, feeding him soup made from herbs, cooling him off with a wet towel."

Aunt Kena looked up at him, nodding at the memory. "You were very sick for a long time, Miss Pîyesî. That was a terrible fever. We almost lost you."

"But you didn't lose me then, Aunt Kena. You brought me back. You healed me. And then you got sick yourself."

"I did, didn't I," Kena said softly. "That was a terrible sickness. Took a long time for me to get better."

"But you did get better," Billy said. "You beat it back. And you'll do the same thing with the diabetes because no matter what happens to you or how sick you get, you always will be a great healer of our people."

She was quiet for several seconds. Then she mumbled incoherently.

Billy thought he had lost her again, but then she shouted, "Okay!" and slammed her hand on the coffee table, sending a loud and large crack through the Formica surface and compressed wood underneath.

She pushed herself up off the couch, rising to her feet like an angry matriarchal elephant getting ready to protect her herd. She stretched her arms, the bones in her shoulders and elbows cracking. She took a deep breath, and Billy heard a snap of wind as she inhaled all the air from the teepee and the surrounding community into her lungs. The animals outside the teepee started to sing, shout and howl; the birds, the small mammals, the coyotes and wolves, the moose, elk and buffalo, all of them, predator and prey, joining together in a song of battle.

Aunt Kena squeezed her hands into fists and snapped her elbows to her side, exhaling a sharp gust of air. The earth seemed to bounce once with her movement. It was as if a goddess had woken up.

When she looked at Dale, she seemed thirty years younger, her face alive and ready to fight. "Okay, let's go," she said with strong conviction. "What do you want me to do?"

Billy jumped up, a smile on his face. "We need to save Dale."

"You said that," she said, her voice booming like Zeus on Mount Olympus. "What exactly do you want me to do?"

Billy took a deep breath and gazed into his aunt's eyes; they reflected fire. "I need you to drive his truck."

Aunt Kena seemed to deflate at hearing his words, and she returned to her usual self. She looked at Billy, her face pleading, now thirty years older again. When she spoke, Billy could barely hear her. "Oh, I don't think I could do that. Dale doesn't really like anybody else to drive his truck."

Twenty-eight

It took a long time for Aunt Kena to walk the half mile to Dale's truck, and even longer to get into the truck. She was a big woman in girth, but she was also shorter than average. It took her at least three attempts to step up onto the running board in order to prepare to squeeze into the truck.

Unlike an average-size person who could just slide onto the truck seat, Aunt Kena had to balance on the running board and determine how to maneuver her bulk onto the driver's seat. She stood on the running board precariously, thinking about her options. She almost lost her balance and fell to the ground, but she managed to catch herself. Still, the truck rocked back and forth as she shifted her weight. The sudden movement threatened to knock her to the ground, so she made the snap decision of entering the truck butt first.

The old aunt sat her expansive derriere on the luxurious leather seats, taking the pressure off her arms and preventing her from falling out. But her stubby legs hung out the door, her hip throbbing with pain. She tried to turn her body and slide farther onto the seat but it was positioned too far forward and the steering wheel blocked her. Dale was a big man, with a large gut, so the seat and steering wheel were set for his frame. But there still wasn't enough room for Aunt Kena to get in.

She tried again and again to push herself behind the steering wheel, but she couldn't jam herself into that tiny space. "I can't do it, Billy," she shouted in frustration. "I can't get in far enough to drive this damn thing."

"You gotta move the seat back, and then adjust the steering wheel," Billy said. He stood a few feet away from the truck door, looking on helplessly because he couldn't help her. It was one thing to help Dale fight the gang members; it was another to manhandle his aunt. The two Jennings kids stood behind him, laughing at Aunt Kena's struggles. Billy was glad to hear them laugh, but it wasn't helping the situation any.

Aunt Kena nodded at Billy's suggestion and slowly reached down to where she thought the seat adjustment handle was. Her hands flailed blindly against the side of the seat, finding no handles, only a bunch of buttons. She pushed at the buttons, but nothing happened.

"Lousy Ford, piece of crap. Stupid truck's broken already!" she shouted. "These buttons don't work."

Billy sighed in exasperation. "They're electronic buttons, Aunt Kena. They won't work unless you start the truck."

She shook her head and muttered a curse. "Okay, then, where are the damn keys?"

"In the ignition. Dale always leaves them in the ignition."

Aunt Kena rolled her eyes. "Something's not right with that boy. Leaving his keys in an expensive truck like this. It's like leaving a pile of money on the porch of your house. Stupid boy," she said, shaking her head. She grunted and groaned, stretching her arm and twisting her body in a vain attempt to reach the keys.

"I can't get at them, Billy."

"You gotta find some way to get at them, Aunt Kena, or Dale's going to die. I'd help you but I can't 'cuz…"

"Yeah, yeah, 'cuz you're dead. I know, I know." she said, cutting him off. "Leave me alone for a second and let me think."

"We don't have a lot of time, Aunt Kena."

"Okay, avert your eyes, everyone, this ain't gonna be pretty." She moaned with effort and lifted up her feet and legs to give her more leverage. She wiggled her body back and forth, which caused her dress to rise up.

Billy quickly turned away so as not get an image that would haunt him for all eternity in the spirit world. The two Jennings kids laughed even harder.

After more grunts and groans from his aunt, Billy heard the truck roar to life. His elation was short-lived though, as the blaring of angry white suburban hip-hop exploded out of the speakers, followed immediately by Aunt Kena's screams of horror.

"Oh my God, what the heck is that noise? Please make it stop. Make it stop, make it stop!"

"It's just Dale's music, Aunt Kena. Just reach over and turn it off."

Kena's arm flailed about, pushing as many buttons as she could reach. The air conditioner blared to life, the windshield washers jumped back and forth and the hazard lights blinked on and off by the time she managed to push the button for the stereo.

The music stopped abruptly, the silence almost deafening, save for the flip flapping of the wipers and the clicking of the hazards. Aunt Kena breathed a sigh of relief. She grabbed the steering wheel with one hand, and with great effort, pulled herself to a seated position. She barely could see over the steering wheel, and her feet couldn't reach the pedals. She adjusted the seat until her toes touched the gas pedal. She pressed her foot on the gas, and the engine roared.

Her face was full of determination. "Get in," she said to Billy.

Billy willed himself into the truck, finding himself in the passenger seat a half second later. If Aunt Kena was surprised by his sudden disappearance and reappearance, she gave no indication. She just pushed her elbows to her side and gripped the gearshift.

Pressing her toes onto the gas pedal as hard as she could, she jerked the truck into drive. The tires spun on the gravel briefly, and then the truck jumped forward.

Billy was supposedly unaffected by the physics of the old world, but the sudden movement forced him back onto his seat. He looked into the rearview mirror and saw the two Jennings kids waving at the truck as it pulled away, leaving behind a trail of dust.

"I can't see too well, so you're going to have to be my navigator," Aunt Kena said. "So where the heck is my stupid nephew?"

"He's probably at the same spot where I was killed."

"You sure about that?" Aunt Kena said, keeping her gaze forward. "You gotta be sure."

Billy didn't hesitate. "I'm sure. Matt wants to make a point."

"Okay, then. Let's go stop him." Aunt Kena gunned the truck even more, reaching for the stereo dial. She turned it on, the music of Eminem screaming into her ears. She turned the volume down, but only slightly.

"You know, this guy's voice sounds like crap, and he's annoying," she said, "but I like the beat, Dick. It's good for dancing and driving."

"My name is Billy, Aunt Kena," Billy said, confused and worried.

"I know that, you idiot. I was talking to Dick Clark."

Billy had no idea who Dick Clark was, or why Aunt Kena was talking to him about music.

Twenty-nine

Now why is Matt driving into Twin Bridges? was Dale's first thought when Matt turned onto the road leading to the old hangout.

This is a crime scene; he shouldn't be doing that. But then Dale realized that he was an idiot. Of course Matt knew this place was a crime scene; he was the one who committed the crime at the scene. He was the one who had killed Billy. And if nothing happened to change things in the next few minutes, Dale would be dead, too.

But if he got shot in the same place that Billy was killed, the police would know something was up. The cops would start a major investigation and would find Gar, who would tell them about Grant who in turn would tell them about Matt and how he killed…

Wait a sec, Dale thought. *Grant wasn't involved, so how could he tell anybody about Matt? It must have been Matt who asked Gar to drop the gun off at the company office while Grant was in Mexico.*

Dale had to figure out how Matt did that and ask him why he killed Billy in the first place. Sure, it probably wouldn't make much difference because Dale would be dead as well. Which wasn't a good thing in the long run, but at least he would know, and he could tell Billy in person, or in ghost, or whatever he was. And if Billy solved the mystery of his death, maybe his spirit would be at peace, and he'd be able to cross over to the spirit world, or heaven, or whatever that place was.

And since he would know who had killed him and why, Dale thought, he wouldn't have to hang around this world and could cross over to wherever Billy had crossed over. They could hang out, which would be kind of cool because Dale never got the chance to get to know his cousin, and Billy was a decent guy, for a dead guy.

But despite discovering there was actually a life after death, Dale didn't want to die. He liked living in the real world, and after he had taken out Gar and his gang in the bar, his life would have been so much better. Everyone would think he was a true badass, a tough mofo who nobody could threaten lest they feel his wrath. And he didn't even have to prove any of his so-called skills and bad-assery because he, with the help of Billy, had already done that. People had seen, heard and felt him in action so nobody was going to tempt that kind of fate again. If he made it out of this mess alive, his life was going to be totally sweet.

But the big question on Dale's mind was when to ask Matt to explain his evil plan. He had seen countless films in which the bad guy spent almost one-quarter of the movie explaining his evil plot to the hero. But he had never seen a movie where the hero asked the bad guy to explain his plans and the bad guy had complied.

Dale thought he might be in one of those films, where the good guy gets killed and no justice is done. But he had to try to get Matt to reveal his evil plot. He decided that after Matt told him to get out of the truck and poked him in the back with the barrel of the gun and they walked single-file to the spot where Billy's body had been found, Dale would ask Matt why he killed Billy. Dale didn't need to know why Matt was going to kill him; that was self-explanatory.

And in the end, it was way too easy. Dale just asked Matt straight out while they were walking to the ravine. "Why'd you kill Billy?" And Matt told him.

"Billy was a good friend, but he was also an idiot," Matt said, obviously not acting like some kind of evil genius. "He should have known better, he should have realized that if he released the information about the high emission rates and the water samples and tried to tie it to the increased rates of cancer, that everyone would hate him for it. He thought he was doing good and helping out those kids and their families, but in reality he was only hurting them and a bunch of other families."

"But someone needed to know what happened to those kids and why."

"No, they didn't. Nobody would really care anyway. I mean, who really cares if a bunch of stupid Indians die? They didn't care when Robert Pickton killed a bunch of

Native women in BC, and they're not going to care if a resource company may have killed them here. Maybe for a week or two it might make the news, but then it's back to business as usual."

"But maybe someone would care this time and do something about it," Dale said, knowing deep in his heart it wasn't true.

Matt laughed. "Yeah, right. And the buffalo might one day return, too. Get your head of the sand, Dale. No one's going to do anything about the report because no one wants to lose all the money and the jobs that the resource company gives us. And if that happened, things would be worse than a couple of kids dying. I'd lose my job and wouldn't be able to feed and house my kids. And so would a lot of other people. The band wouldn't get any money from the company, and the community center, the aquatic center and the school you went to would all fall apart. We'd never get new houses, our infrastructure would crumble and we'd become like one of those poor reserves in northern Ontario that don't have anything. We'd complain about not having any running water, and our elders and children would die of Third World diseases. We'd beg and plead for the government to help us. Is that what you want?"

Dale didn't want any of that to happen, but he also didn't want kids dying because of resource exploration and exploitation with nothing being done about it. As they headed down into the ravine toward the creek bed, Dale thought about running and trying to escape. But he knew his chances were slim. His muscles ached because of the action at the bar last night. And he was smart enough to know that not even the greatest Hollywood action hero can outrun a bullet.

So he kept talking to Matt, stalling for time and hoping against hope that something would happen and he would be saved. The odds were against some sort of divine intervention, but he had to try.

"So if no one really cares about Native kids dying because of oil exploration and development and sour gas wells, then why did you kill Billy when he threatened to release the information about the high emissions?"

Matt laughed again. "You know how much it costs any corporation when something like this happens? Sure, in the end, nothing really changes; the company still gets the oil or the gold or whatever they're digging for. But only because they've put a lot of money into damage control, public relations and communication strategy. They also have to grease political wheels, and that also costs money. Sometimes more intense monitoring systems or highly expensive environmental protection equipment and procedures are put in place to show that they care for the well-being of the earth and the people who live near the developments. And that stuff is expensive and has a major effect on the bottom line. Shareholders don't like it when the bottom line is affected. It really hurts the return on their RSPs."

"So that's why you killed Billy? Because your RSP might be affected?"

"No, because everyone's RSPs would be affected. Man, you're just like your cousin, stupid and shortsighted. Can't see the big picture. And the big picture is that profits count a lot more than the lives of a few kids. And one or two dudes like you. It's a simple fact of life in the real world."

They arrived at the bottom of the ravine, and Matt tapped Dale on the shoulder. "Okay, stop here. This is perfect," he said, as if he was just picking out the ideal picnic site. "Turn around."

Dale did what he was told. He tried to look Matt in the eye but he couldn't; he was fixated on the barrel of the gun that was pointed at him.

But Matt wasn't ready to shoot him; he still wanted to talk. "Billy's big mistake was that he was stupid. He thought he could change the world. He didn't know that by letting me know what he was going to do, I was going to tell Grant, and Grant was going to tell me to handle it."

"Grant told you to kill Billy?" Dale asked, astonished

"Not in so many words," Matt said with a shrug. "He just told me to take care of the situation. To make sure it was dead and buried before he returned from his Mexican holiday. He also told me my job was on the line."

"So you killed Billy to protect your job."

"No! I killed Billy to protect my family!" Matt shouted in anger. "I got three kids to feed and to put through school, and I wanna make sure they get all the good things in life I didn't get. And Billy's actions were threatening all of that. I tried to talk him out of it, make him see the big picture, but he was just too focused on those two little kids. So I had to do something. And I did."

Dale shook his head sadly, realizing that this was what his people had become. So focused on jobs and money that they would go to any lengths to protect it. But who could blame them? They didn't make this world, but they had to live in it and survive somehow. Even so, Dale couldn't believe the next words that came out of his mouth,

"You'll never get away with it," he said, like some pathetic action hero in a B-rated action movie.

Matt laughed. "Of course I'll get away with it. I've already gotten away with Billy's death, and yours will make things even easier for me. Because of what happened at the bar last night, everyone will think the gang killed you. And after that, they'll pin Billy's death on them, too. Easy peasy."

Dale sighed. Matt was right, pretty much on all counts. He hoped it wouldn't hurt to die. And that his spirit wasn't left behind to talk to only Aunt Kena; that was too much like his real life.

Suddenly, a loud screech and a flash of black interrupted Dale's thoughts. It was an odd sound for a pistol to make, but then Dale realized the sound wasn't coming from the gun.

The screeching was coming from a crow, and it was attacking Matt. The bird flew at Matt's head, pecking the top of his skull. Matt jumped away, screaming. He was also waving the gun around, and Dale ducked and dodged, hoping it wouldn't accidently go off and kill him.

The bird then attacked Matt's hands, flapping its wings and pecking at his skin, apparently trying to make him drop the gun.

Dale turned and started to run. He took about three steps when he tripped over an exposed tree root and fell flat on his face. His glasses and his hat flew from his head, and he turned onto his back, stunned and in even more pain than before.

The bird continued to squawk and peck at Matt, who yelled and tried to swipe the bird away. Then a shot blast, an explosion that shook the entire area and deafened Dale. A second later, another shot rang out. Black feathers spotted with blood floated down from the sky.

Matt stood over Dale, pointing the pistol at his head. Matt's face was red from scratches, and he also had several scratches on his hands. He didn't say a word; he just shook his head and pulled the trigger.

There was no explosion, just a simple click. Matt looked at the gun with a frown. Then he pointed it at Dale and pulled the trigger. Again only a click. He repeated the action over and over again, at least six times, but nothing happened.

"Stupid freaking gun," Matt said looking at the pistol again. "I need more ammo."

He bent down and swung the gun against Dale's temple.

Dale saw a flash of light; he felt a searing pain and then nothing but blackness.

Thirty

When Dale came to, he saw Billy standing over him. He was smiling. And then he gave Dale a nod.

"Billy," Dale said, raising his arm.

But then Billy's face was replaced by another. It was the Mountie, Constable Sara. She was leaning in looking at Dale, extreme worry etched on her face.

"Dale," she said, with some panic in her voice. "Are you okay? Did you get shot?"

"Matt…" The word could barely come out of his mouth. "He…he pistol…whipped me. Then he went to get more bullets…"

Dale began to panic, looking around for Matt.

"Matt, Matt!" he shouted. He had to warn Constable Sara of the danger; she was too pretty to get shot. He tried to push himself up, but the effort was too much for his injured body to take. The world began to spin, and he felt himself falling onto his back again.

Constable Sara quickly grabbed the back of his head to ensure it didn't hit the ground.

"Whoa, take it easy, big fella. You don't have to worry about Matt. He's dead." Her voice was so soft and her touch behind his head so soothing that he had no choice but to take it easy. But what she said was confusing.

"Matt's dead? When did that happen?"

"I don't know. We got the call about twenty minutes ago. He was run over."

"Run over? By who?"

"Some big Native woman. Says she's your auntie."

"Aunt Kena?"

"That's the lady."

"Aunt Kena ran over Matt? How did she do…?" A sick feeling came over Dale, worse than the thought of being shot in the head. His head began to swim again, but it had nothing to do with being pistol-whipped.

"Was she driving a blue F-150?" he asked, taking a deep swallow.

"Yeah. Although it's going to need a lot of work. It seems Matt was standing by his truck when she drove into the area. She didn't stop, and he got squished between the trucks. Let's just say it wasn't a pretty sight."

"Oh, my truck, my beautiful truck," Dale groaned. He knew he could probably get everything fixed, but his truck would never be the same. There was probably hidden damage to the suspension or the axles that he wouldn't notice till months or even years later. And then there was Matt; a new paint job could never hide the blood.

"You shouldn't worry about your truck," the constable said. "Your aunt saved your life. If she hadn't drove into Matt, he would have reloaded his gun and shot you, the same way he shot Billy."

Dale knew she was right, but he loved his truck. And now it was a piece of junk with bits of blood and body parts all over it. He sighed.

Constable Sara pulled him up to a sitting position and then she stood up. "Come on, you seem to be fine. Let's get you up and out of here."

"Shouldn't I wait for the paramedics to check on me?"

"Nah, you can meet them up on the road." She bent down, grabbed his hands and pulled him to his feet. She was plenty strong. Dale staggered slightly so she put her arm around him to help him stay steady. "Besides, based on what I heard about what happened last night, you can take care of yourself pretty well."

Dale had no idea what she was talking about. But then he recalled how Billy had helped him take out the gang-bangers and then knock Gar on his back. He did a mental fist pump—*Yes!*—as he realized the story was getting around. He was one badass mofo.

"I mean, not only did you challenge Gar on his own territory, but you also took him and some of his boys out," she said as they walked up the ravine with Dale leaning against her more than he really needed to. "I didn't believe the story at first, but witnesses said it was true. Somebody even videoed part of the fight on a smartphone and uploaded it to YouTube."

Dale couldn't believe his luck. Now, no one could deny who he was and what he did to Gar and his boys because there was actual footage of him in action.

"I was just angry because I thought they had killed Billy," Dale said with mock humility. "I guess I probably owe those boys an apology since they had nothing to do with it."

"I wouldn't recommend that. And I wouldn't condone you doing that again," she said harshly. "We take a dim view of vigilante justice, no matter if it's deserved or not." But then her voice became softer. "Although, I must admit I'm pretty impressed with what you did. You seem to have a lot of hidden talents, and I'm sorry if I thought bad things about you in the past. You have some great qualities, and I should have seen those."

This day just keeps getting better and better, Dale thought. He wondered what the etiquette was for asking a cop for her phone number at a crime scene. Was it frowned upon? Or did it happen all the time? Based on what she had just said, maybe she wouldn't mind?

But Dale never got the chance. One of the paramedics saw them and ran over. He somewhat roughly steered him away from Sara, toward the waiting ambulance. Dale glanced over his shoulder, and Sara smiled at him.

He tried to smile back, but the muscle movement hurt his face. He was glad he wouldn't have to fight anymore because it was hard work, and painful. Of course, he was aware that without Billy's help, he couldn't fight. But then again, he didn't really have to.

The paramedic set Dale down on the bumper of the ambulance bay and began to work on him. He used wet cotton swabs to dab at the injuries from Matt's pistol-whipping. The pain of the cleansing liquid stung. Dale winced but didn't want to give the paramedic the satisfaction of seeing that he was in pain.

A voice from a distance called him. Instantly he knew it was Aunt Kena because she was the only one who called him that. She was lumbering toward him. She had stitches on her face and hands, and she looked angry.

"Where have you been, Eyikos?" she shouted at him. "I need a ride home."

Dale didn't look around for his truck because he didn't want to see the damage. That was something he wasn't ready to deal with at the moment. "I can't give you a ride home."

"Someone's got to give me a ride. Bingo starts in a couple of hours, and I don't want to miss a number."

"I'm not sure you're going to make it home for that, Aunt Kena. Some things are more important than bingo."

She gave him a look as if he had spit at her. "Watch your mouth, boy. Just get me a ride home. And I need some tomatoes. The ones you got me last week went bad too fast. And oranges. They're good for my bones. And some chocolate too, so I don't get tired."

"I'll do what I can, Aunt Kena. I'm a bit busy at the moment."

"Me too. I hope you don't forget that I just saved your life."

He sighed and looked at his aunt. For the first time in his life, he actually looked at her. Sure, she was fat and old, but he saw sparks of fire in her eyes. And he realized that sometime in her life, when she was much younger, she had probably been the most beautiful woman on the Rez. He smiled at her.

"Yeah, I heard about that. Thanks," he said softly.

She waved his comment away and sat down on the bumper next to him. The entire ambulance tilted downward with her weight. She placed her hand gently on his shoulder, and all the pain from the fight and the pistol-whipping faded away. The look on Dale's face gave away his amazement. She truly did have healing powers.

"Don't mention it," she said. "Sometimes us elders have to come to your aid when you young folks are in trouble. Maybe I should have helped sooner, I don't know."

"You did what you could, Aunt Kena," Dale said. "And that was a lot."

She nodded and looked about the field. There were tears in her eyes. "I killed a man, Eyikos," she said sadly.

"I know, but he was going to kill me. And he killed Billy. So look at it instead as saving my life. I'll never forget it."

She nodded, and after a moment, she slapped him on the shoulder. "You better not forget it. I saved your worthless life!"

"I won't," he said with a laugh. "You'll never let me."

Dale wanted to ask his Aunt Kena one question, but he couldn't figure out how to approach it. He wasn't sure if she even knew the answer.

"He's gone," she said, as if she'd read his mind. "Miss Pîyesî, I mean, Billy, left us."

"Did he…?" was all Dale could say before he choked up.

Aunt Kena nodded. "Yep. And he took his little birdie friend with him."

"That crow!" Dale's eyes lit up with joy. "I thought the crow was dead. Matt shot it."

"You can't kill one of those. They are powerful and dangerous creatures."

"Just like you. And like you, that crow saved my life. It attacked Matt, stopping him from shooting me."

"Hmm," was all Aunt Kena said. Then she added, "Even so, dangerous and powerful. Not good to hang out with folks like that."

"Yeah, I'll remember that the next time."

Aunt Kena gave him a surprised look. "There's going to be a next time?"

"I hope not, but I was thinking about quitting my job and moving back to the Rez."

"With me?"

"No, not with you, I was going to get my own place."

"That wasn't an invitation, Eyikos. I was just worried you were thinking about it."

"I was also thinking about opening some kind of business in the village. You know, some kind of agency to help people who need help. I have a rep now, you know. People will respect me."

"But first you got to get me a ride home," she said, returning to her usual cranky self. "Then you got to buy me some tomatoes, oranges and chocolate. And none of that dark chocolate, that stuff tastes terrible, not sweet at all."

Dale sighed, wondering if he should just stay in the city. Opening an agency and living on the Rez near his Aunt Kena might be harder than he thought.

Thirty-one

Two weeks after Matt's death, Grant sat at his desk, doing paperwork for two upcoming projects. The first had to do with the development of several new well sites. The wells would be drilled to access more of the sour gas beneath the land on the Rez. He knew residents might raise a stink because the new wells would be much closer to the village than any of the others. In fact, the sites were only a few miles from the school, which would probably raise the hackles of the people opposed to such things

In a way, Grant agreed with their concerns. He wouldn't want someone drilling for sour gas near his kids' school. It was not just the risk of a possible accident that bothered him or an emissions leak. The effects of sour gas on groundwater was the real worry, that's what the studies always said. The negative effects included a decline in health, mental acuity and the development of tumors and other forms of cancer. And then there was the noise of the drilling and the well itself when the drilling was complete, plus the electromagnetic field that this type of exploration created.

But Grant thought that if these people didn't want to subject their kids to this kind of stuff, they shouldn't have built the school near the site of future wells. Approvals for these sites were given almost a decade ago, but the company delayed drilling because of the downturn in the economy. It was believed the approvals had lapsed within ten years, because the company never mentioned or complained about the new school being built so close to possible future development.

The drilling created good jobs for the community, and if it was one thing these people needed, it was good jobs.

Besides, the company paid for half of the school anyway, so the people didn't really have a right to complain.

Grant was also working on the approval process for the new pipeline coming through the area. It was one of the company's biggest in its history. Stretching from the Arctic to Texas, the pipeline would take oil, gas and oil sands bitumen to the major U.S. markets. So many Native bands were affected that Grant had lost count. His particular role on this Rez was only a small part of the entire process, but it was hoped that when the pipeline was built, it would spark development of a bitumen processing mine on the northern edge of the Rez.

The geologists had shown that there was a decent oil sands deposit in the area, not as big as the ones near Fort

Mac, so it wasn't worth the effort to exploit it. But when the pipeline came through…well, all bets were off.

It was hard work, but the projects ensured a future for Grant, his family and DBA Resources.

Then the phone in his office rang. It was a bit weird because all of his calls were supposed to come through Jamie, the receptionist.

This one came directly to him.

Grant picked it up. "Hello."

"Yes, Grant, do you know who this is?" said a man's voice, sounding like some friendly guy from a kid's show who had puppets and liked to play dress-up.

Grant recognized the voice. It was the chairman of the Board of Directors for the parent company. He stiffened, worried about what to say. It was like getting a phone call from God.

"Are you there, Grant?" the voice said.

"Yes. Yes, sir, I am here. I'm sorry, I was just…"

"Yes, about these incidents," the chairman said, cutting Grant off, not really caring about the apology. "The board is very concerned about the situation out there."

Grant swallowed. It was never a good idea to attract the attention of the Board of Directors, even for good work. Because then they paid more attention to you. If you did good work, they could be very pleased and could reward you in many ways. But if they were concerned or even displeased, that could be very bad.

Grant had heard stories of people who displeased the Board of Directors. If they were lucky, they were fired and never again allowed to work in the industry, even for a competing company. But if they were unlucky, well, Grant shuddered just thinking about it. He had heard about horrible industrial accidents in which the person severely injured or even killed had recently displeased the Board of Directors.

"No, things are progressing smoothly," he said, putting on a brave voice.

"Two violent deaths in the space of a couple of days doesn't sound like smooth progress to me. How about you?"

"No, it doesn't, but the second death played perfectly into our hands. It wrapped up the investigation into the first death nice and neat, with nothing pointing to us as being involved."

"Yes, that is true," the chairman said after a pause. "But it was a bit messy. We are not big fans of messy."

"Sometimes things have to get messy to work," Grant said, not believing he was being this direct with the chairman. But he was still feeling a confident high on how the whole mess with Matt and Billy had turned out. With Matt now dead, no one would know that it was the company or himself that prompted Matt to "take care of things."

"That's how the whole business works, doesn't it," Grant continued. "Extracting oil and gas from the earth is a messy business, but in the end, it all works out for the company."

There was a pause on the other end of the line, and for a moment, Grant thought the chairman had cut off the conversation.

But he hadn't ended the call. "You make a decent point, Grant," the chairman said. "It did work out very well for us, although luck played a role. The board is going to keep an eye on this area for a while. We've got some major plans, so we'll be sending one of our direct representatives out there to keep a watch on things. Is that okay with you?"

Grant knew he wasn't really being asked permission, but he was also stunned. He had never met a direct representative of the board in person. Or maybe he had and never knew it. They were legendary in the company—part accountant, part black ops security personnel.

"That sounds great," Grant said with as much enthusiasm as he could muster. But deep down he was experiencing some serious acid reflux. "I can't wait to welcome him or her."

"Oh, you won't meet our representative. But that person will be there nonetheless," said the chairman. "And what about that strange man with the incredible fighting skills?"

"Oh, you mean Dale. We don't have to worry about him. He's harmless."

"He doesn't seem harmless," the chairman snapped. "He took out six of our associates in about ten seconds."

"They weren't really associates of ours, just some hired help," Grant said. "Although I must admit they weren't that great as hired help."

"Yes, but I hear this fellow is moving into the community to open up a private detective agency. That's a bit troubling."

"Then you'll be glad to know I have the matter under control, sir. Even though Dale has some surprising strengths, he does have one weakness. He has a fondness for an old aunt of his. If he causes trouble for us, we'll cause some trouble for her. Tit for tat."

"Good then," the chairman said. And then this time he disconnected the call.

Grant set down the receiver, breathing a sigh of relief. Dale likely wouldn't cause the company anymore trouble. But if he did, Aunt Kena better watch out.

Thirty-two

Billy was alone in the circle, the arches made out of birch saplings reaching up to meet over his head. He stood there, confused about why he was in this place and how he got there. He tried to remember, but all he had was a vision of his cousin Dale lying on the ground with a bit of blood trickling down the side of his face. Somehow Billy knew Dale was alive. And Dale was smiling. First at Billy and then at a pretty woman who had come to see if he was all right.

Billy was glad Dale was fine because Dale was a really good guy. A bit of a geek and a poser, but that was who he was. That didn't make him less good.

But that memory didn't explain what he was doing here, standing under the frame of a sweat lodge. It had been years since he had participated in a sweat and much longer since he had made one.

The last time had been with his Mosum.

"What you doing just standing there?" his Mosum shouted at him. "I thought you were going to help me?"

Billy turned quickly, surprised at the sound of the old man's voice. It had been such a long time since he'd heard it. Or was it? He couldn't remember. Things were a little fuzzy at the moment.

But he was ecstatic to see his Mosum. He ran to the old man, and when they collided, Billy wrapped his arms as tight as he could around him. Billy's arms were too short to reach around the old man's bearlike frame, but he tried.

"Whoa, whoa!" Mosum said with a laugh, hugging the boy back. "What's the big deal?"

"I missed you," Billy said, tears in his eyes.

"I was only gone for a little bit," Mosum said. "I only went into the garage to check on a few things."

"But it seemed like a long time. A really long time."

Mosum stepped back and looked down at Billy. He ruffled his hair. "Yeah, I guess to someone as young as you, time does move more slowly. What's a short time for me must be a long time for you," the old man said. "But listen, I have to head out somewhere this afternoon. I won't be away long, but you're going to have to finish the rest of the lodge without me."

"You're leaving again? But you just got back."

"I never really left; you know that."

Billy thought about what his Mosum said, and he was right; his Mosum had always been there, even when he was gone.

"Okay," he said with a nod.

"And you'll finish the lodge while I'm gone?" Mosum asked.

"I don't know. I've never built one by myself. I'm not sure I'll do it right."

Mosum chuckled. "Hard stuff's done already. The rest is easy. It'll take you a couple of hours at most. You don't need to be a rocket scientist to finish it."

Despite Mosum's confidence in him, Billy was unsure he could complete the structure without help. His uneasiness must have shown on his face.

"Hey, don't worry about it. It's easy; all right?" Mosum said with a smile. "You remember seeing those blankets and tarps in the garage, when you went to get that carpet for the floor?"

Billy nodded, picturing the small pickup truck on blocks.

"Okay, use two tarps to create a skin over the frame of the sweat lodge, tying them down at the base of the arches," Mosum continued. "Don't tie them too loose or too tight, just nice and snug. There's plenty of tarp to cover the whole thing. There may be a few little gaps here and there, but that's okay as long as the gaps aren't too big. And try not to cover too much of the door. You got that?"

Billy nodded. It seemed simple as Mosum was explaining it, but hearing instructions and then putting them into action was something else.

The old man continued. "Okay, next, drape all the blankets over the tarp. You don't have to be too fancy, just layer them over and tuck the ones hanging on the ground underneath the base. Do it as best as you can till it looks like everything is sealed. And don't cover the door; just use one of the heavier but small blankets and tuck it under one of the other layers, you know, of the blankets, and let it hang over the opening, just enough so it touches the ground. That all make sense to you?"

Billy nodded, but slowly, reluctantly.

Mosum laughed again and slapped Billy on the shoulder. "Don't worry about it. It'll all make sense when you get out there and start working on it." Mosum walked toward the surrounding woods.

"I'll see you later," he said as he got closer to the edge.

Billy followed him. "Mosum?"

Mosum stopped and turned toward him. "Yeah?"

"Where you going?" Billy asked

"Don't worry, I'll be back later tonight."

"Is everything all right?"

Mosum paused for a bit. "For the most part, yeah, but that's pretty normal around here. See ya later. After we do the sweat, we'll go hunting for buffalo."

"Really? You mean hunting buffalo for real?"

"Oh yeah. We can still do that here. And it's about time you learned how to hunt."

And then Mosum turned away and stepped into the trees. Billy kept his eyes on him as walked away, but he lost him. It was as if the old man had faded into the trees. Billy was worried for a moment, but Mosum did say he would be back real soon. And he'd want the sweat lodge to be done so that in the next day or two, they could actually have a sweat. Billy ran back to the frame and started working.

Mosum was right. The rest was easy, although admittedly, getting the two tarps in place and tying them down so no huge gaps were visible was a bit tricky. Billy worried about getting the correct snugness, and he wasn't sure if the frame could handle the weight. But as he put on blanket after blanket, adding more weight, it held. And the tarps and the blankets seemed to distribute the weight evenly so that all the arches were handling the load as a group. It him took a few attempts to get the blanket over the door right—it fell to the ground on his first few efforts or didn't completely cover the opening. But finally he got the blanket to hang properly, and his job was done.

Billy stepped back, admiring his work. He felt an urge to step through the opening to see what it was like inside, but it didn't seem like the right thing to do. He'd enter during the sweat when he was invited to enter…if he was invited.

He shook the thought away. Of course he would be invited; he was old enough, and he had built the lodge himself. Maybe he could invite others. He remembered that a couple of kids hung around with his Aunt Kena. They'd be perfect for this sweat. But he wasn't sure if he could get a hold of her because she lived so far away. There must be someway to contact her. But he decided not to worry about that because even though he knew he would probably go back and help Aunt Kena, Dale and his people, that was sometime in the future, and something he couldn't control. He would worry about it when the time came.

Right now, in the present, there was the lodge. It didn't seem like much; it leaned slightly, but Billy had built it on his own. A few days ago there was nothing on this patch of ground, and now, because of him, a sweat lodge stood before him, looking as if a group of women at a quilting bee had stitched it together.

His arms were sore, and his hands were spotted with dried blood from burst blisters. His back and shoulders ached from not being used in this manner for many years, but it was good pain. Pain that he welcomed and appreciated because it was the by-product of creating something positive.

Epilogue

Bear walked into the woods looking for something. He found an old stump filled with ants and figured that was what he was looking for. He started digging at the stump, scooping away chunks of dead wood and dirt in order to get at the tasty ants inside. Thousands upon thousands of warrior ants, and even more worker ants, attacked him, biting him countless times, but his fur was so thick that Bear wasn't affected by their efforts. He lapped at the insects, devouring thousands with every lick. He could have eaten the entire colony—eggs, larvae, queen, every last one of them. And it would have satisfied his appetite, made him relaxed enough to take a nice long nap in the summer sun.

Bear loved the summer sun, its place in the sky, its heat, its yellowness. So much better than the cold orange sun in the fall that couldn't warm a squirrel much less a massive brown bear like him. But he knew that he would anger the other ants if he ate the entire ant colony.

Ants were tenacious insects, simple in design, but because of their large numbers, they were almost indestructible. Humans joked that at the end of nuclear war, the only species to survive would be Keith Richards and cockroaches. But the cockroaches wouldn't survive because the ants would eat them, turning them into some sort of insect herd, like cattle, breeding and controlling them as the key food source through the long nuclear winter.

And because of their huge numbers and the fact that ants existed before the dinosaurs, ants had long memories. They didn't mind other animals preying on them—they did the same. But if Bear ate an entire colony, queen and all, the other colonies would hear about it. And they would remember the genocide, holding the memory for a long time, letting it fester for years, decades, even millennia before acting.

Ants could hold a grudge for a very long time. And they were organized. During any winter hibernation, they could gather all their colonies and convince some of the other small-brained animals such as birds, rodents and pack animals such as wolves, coyotes and bison, into a revolt.

So Bear ate the ants, but he didn't gorge himself.

Crow flew in and landed on a tree branch above Bear. He watched Bear with amusement. To get the large mammal's attention, the bird let go a bit of white poop that landed on a nearby log.

Bear jumped back in surprise, shouting, "Hey!"

He looked for the source of the "attack" and spotted the bird. Bear frowned.

"That wasn't nice," he said. "You could have just called out to get my attention."

"I didn't think you'd hear me. You were so intent on your ants, and I knew you were thinking about whether they were planning a revolt this year. So that's why I pooped."

"Well, it was completely unnecessary."

"I don't think so," Crow said, haughtily. He flew down to a lower branch nearer to Bear, but out of reach of his long claws. "But do you want to hear a secret about ants?"

Bear, picking a few stray ants from its teeth, claws and fur and popping them into his mouth, nodded vigorously.

"The thing about ants," Crow began in a whisper, causing Bear to lean forward, "is that they're *always* planning a revolt. They can't help it; it's in their nature."

Bear slumped down in disappointment, falling to a seating position. "That's not funny," he said, dejected.

"It's *very* funny," Crow said. "It's funny because it's *so* true."

Bear waved a meaty paw at the bird, not as an attack, just dismissing the words. "So you're back?"

"Yes, I'm back."

"And it all worked out?"

The bird shrugged slightly. "Seems like it. One boy is dead, has accepted his death and is on his way to the Happy Hunting grounds. Meanwhile, the other is alive, and your relative Kena has accepted her role as a respected elder again. She is no longer hiding from her powers and her responsibility."

Crow fluttered down from his branch and landed on Bear's shoulder. A lone worker ant skittered across the bear's fur so the bird pecked at it and swallowed it.

"And the best part," Crow continued, "is that the bad guy is no longer around. Evil has been vanquished, and all is right with the world again."

Bear sighed. "I hope so."

"Everything isn't right in the world? Then why the heck did I go through all that trouble with Billy, Dale and the gang?"

"No, no. Things are better now. And you played an important role in helping Billy, Dale and Kena find their way. Without you, their success would not be possible so I am extremely grateful."

"Enough that I've paid my debt?"

Bear chuckled. "Close, but not quite."

"Figured as much," Crow said. "But I can live with that for the moment."

Bear got up from his seated position and started to lumber toward the trees in search of something else to eat. Maybe some honey, like the bears in fairytales. Honey was always good, and bees weren't as bright as ants. Each hive was like an English football team and hated all the other hives. They would never organize a revolt.

Crow adjusted his position but remained on Bear. He was enjoying the ride. But something was nagging the bird.

"So even though things are better, things aren't completely right with the world?" Crow said.

"No, they are not," Bear said sadly. "We're moving in the right direction, but we still have a long way to go. We've defeated only a small part of the evil that has infected the world. The major part of it is much bigger, more dangerous to root out. And unlike ants, this group won't forgive if you only eat or remove a small part of its colony.

"This is a greedy vindictive creature, made worse by the fact that its roots come from the soul of humanity itself."

"That's going to be tough to get rid of," Crow said, thoughtfully. "Impossible, some would say."

"And they may be correct, but we still have to try."

Bear, with the bird still on his shoulder, walked on in silence. Finally, Crow stretched his wings and flew up to a branch on a nearby tree.

"So you'll probably need me to go back sometime in the near future."

"Yes, I will need your help again. And this time, I will not demand it to pay a debt. I will ask you as a friend to help me."

The bird twisted his head to look more closely at Bear. His comment was something new and completely unexpected. Crow's response was also new and unexpected.

"Then I will help you."

Bear nodded. "But not now. Go get some rest. Fly free for a while knowing that you have my gratitude."

Crow nodded. He moved to fly away, but something held him back. "It's probably going to get worse, isn't it?"

Bear nodded. "It will get very bad. So bad that even I will probably have to cross over."

"That's very bad."

"And it might get to the point where I might have to ask the ants to help."

The bird shivered at the comment. If ants were to get involved, it *must* be bad.

"But not now," Bear said, waving a paw. "Go be with your family and friends. Fly the skies and enjoy yourself. I have no need for your help today."

And with that dismissal, Crow flew off, out of the tree and toward the sun, where the warm updrafts made it easier to fly.